ROCKY GROUND

WENDY SMITH

Edited by CREATING INK

Photography by FURIOUSFOTOG / GOLDEN CZERMAK

Cover Design by FURIOUSFOTOG / GOLDEN CZERMAK

Cover Model NICK PULOS

*CW References to past sexual abuse

1

JESSIE

Of course it's raining on the day of my mother's funeral.

Abigail Lane would be so proud that the heavens opened up and wept at the thought of her demise. She always did want to be important.

The car slows before coming to a stop, and I screw up my face at the rain. Despite my mixed feelings about today, I made an effort to dress nicely for the service, and it would also be typical of my mother to make a mess of my outfit.

The driver opens the door and holds out his hand. I take it, step out onto the sidewalk, and give him a small smile as he hands me an umbrella.

"Thank you. I should have thought."

He shakes his head. "I always carry one in the car, and you'll need it today."

I'm so awful; I can't even remember his name. He did tell me, but he's not wearing a name tag, and I'm not that observant of my manners at the best of times. But he's an older man, at a guess in his sixties, and his smile is kind.

Kindness is the last thing I want today.

"Thank you."

I'm tempted to just get back in the car and have him drive me away. I'm not even sure why I'm honouring her wish to be buried—cremation feels so much more final than this. It's not like she ever took my wishes into consideration.

I tighten the grip on the umbrella and walk up the path toward the grave site, sighing when I have to step off and onto the grass. My six-inch heels sink into the soft ground, and I roll my eyes.

Mom's not worth destroying a thousand-dollar pair of Louboutins for, but I'll take the hit if it means seeing her in the ground.

A group of people have gathered around the grave, and a tall man wearing a suit approaches me as I get closer.

"Jessie Lane? I'm Jamie Mulrose."

I nod. "It's good to meet you."

He extends his hand, and I shake it. This is the first time I've met the funeral director in person—all our discussions have been over the phone. But I wanted my time here to be as brief as possible, and fly in and out.

I'm sure he's wondering why I didn't want a full service. I chose the quickest option. He'll say some words by the grave, she'll get lowered into it, and then I'll leave. Nice and simple.

It shouldn't surprise me that there are people here—I'm sure she's made friends in the ten-plus years since I've seen her. None of them know the real her, the depths that she'd sink to, and my stomach twists at that thought.

But today is about me, and maybe it's selfish to think that, but I don't care. She left me with a ton of baggage I'll be carrying for the rest of my life and never gave me the bare minimum of an apology.

"Let's get started. I'm sure you'll want to get out of the rain." Jamie smiles.

"Yes, please."

We take a few more steps and I'm on steadier ground again with the mats they've laid out around the grave.

"I'll just give you a moment," he says, and gestures to the grave, stepping back as I step closer.

"Thank you."

My nerves are on such a thin thread that it'd be easy to snap over the smallest of things today. I have to try and keep myself under control.

At least for now.

I only have a moment before someone moves in my peripheral vision, and I tighten my grip on my umbrella as a hand rests on my shoulder.

I've never been good with people randomly touching me, but today I guess it's par for the course.

"I'm so sorry for your loss," a woman's voice gently murmurs.

I'm not.

"Thank you."

Relieved when she removes her hand before I shrug it off, I take a step forward toward the hole in the ground my mother is to be lowered into.

Warm rain continues to fall.

The dirt turns to mud, which slides down into the grave.

Usually, I'd think this was depressing, but it seems apt given the mess she made of me.

The service starts, but my eyes are focused on the poplar casket, waiting to be buried. I thought I'd have more peace seeing it, but all it does is stir up the anger that constantly bubbles away inside me.

Slowly, the casket is lowered into the grave, the heavy weight on my chest lifting with each inch that it drops.

A hand lands on my arm, and I flinch before composing myself.

"Did you want to speak, Ms Lane?" the funeral director asks.

I swallow hard. If he hadn't asked, I probably would just have turned and walked away the second we were done. But he requested it. And I'm paying for this shit show.

"Sure. I'll speak."

I don't meet anyone's gaze. I'm sure they're all looking like they feel sorry for me, and that's the last thing they need to do.

"Abigail Lane was the absolute worst person I have ever had the misfortune to know."

Gasps echo around the empty graveyard.

"I'm only here to make sure that she's buried and there's no chance of her coming back." I look down into the grave. "Rot in hell, Mom."

Before anyone can say anything to me, I turn and stalk toward the car.

The driver gets out as I approach, and he takes the umbrella and opens the door for me with a slight nod.

"Thank you," I say as I slide into the back seat. "Can you please take me back to the hotel?"

"Of course." He smiles and closes the door.

It's done. She's gone.

But the damage she did to me will linger forever.

I am my mother's legacy.

"Jessie, it's time to go."

The knot in my stomach grows, but I step into the room and beam the biggest smile I can.

"That's my girl," Mom says.

"Are you sure you're not putting too much pressure on her?" Dad purses his lips.

"Jessie can handle it. She's going to be a star."

Dad's brows knit, and he stands, walking toward me. "But do you want to do this?"

I nod. If I do anything else, Mom will have a meltdown. And Dad doesn't have to be here with her all the time.

"I just want you to be happy, Jessie. You don't have to do this if you don't want to."

"Stop fussing, Seth. Jessie's going to get the commercial and a foot in the door. Our girl is going to be famous."

He frowns. "But does Jessie—"

"Jessie's fine," Mom snaps. "Now let's get going. We have an appointment with her agent at four. If we don't get back in time for dinner, order takeout."

I swallow hard. Last week, I auditioned for a television commercial for a breakfast cereal, and today, my agent will tell me if I've got it. I'm not sure where Mom found him, but the thought of being anywhere near him makes my stomach churn.

I don't know if she notices the way he leers at me, but if she does, she ignores it. All because this is what she wants.

While I love performing, I don't want this.

But saying something will just cause more trouble with her, and I don't want my dad to suffer along with me. They fight enough as it is.

"Well, if you're sure ..." He offers an uncertain smile, and before I know it, Mom's whisked me out of the room and into the car.

"That man," she mutters. "He'll get in the way of our dreams if we let him."

I say nothing, but buckle myself into the passenger seat. By the time we get back, Dad will have drowned his sorrows in a bottle of whiskey, and he won't press the issue again. For today at least.

I'm so lost in memories that I don't notice we've stopped at the hotel until the driver gets out and opens the door.

I stare at him blankly before taking his offered hand and stepping out of the car.

"I'll be here the rest of the night I think, but I'll call if I need you," I say. "I've got an eleven o'clock flight tomorrow morning otherwise."

He nods. "I'll be here to collect you."

"Thank you."

He smiles. I'm sure at home, he has a family. Maybe a wife, children, even grandchildren. Envy sits at the bottom of my stomach like a weight.

There are very few people on this planet who care about me right now.

I miss my friends, but it's my fault I'm alone.

Losing my mother should have created a giant hole in my

life, but the only reason I'm here is because she'd put me down as her next of kin, and someone had to pay for her funeral. I guess she had no one either, but I'm the last person who wants to deal with her death and everything that's come with it.

But, just as I did when I was a kid, I stepped up to the plate and did what I was supposed to do.

When I turned eighteen, my father decided that drinking wasn't the answer. He sobered up enough to take control of the situation, kick out my mother, and support me the way he always should have.

My mother's quest for fame was what screwed me up. It was my dad's parenting that put me on the path to the career I have now.

I have such mixed feelings over Dad's role in my life, but at least he came through for me in the end.

When I reach my room, I slip off my shoes and head straight into a hot shower. It can't wash away the pain, but it makes me feel safe.

Safety is what I crave more than anything else on the planet.

After I'm warm, I towel off and then wrap myself up in a big fluffy hotel bathrobe.

Reaching the couch, I grab my bag, then pull my mobile out and scroll through my contacts.

Dad.

Pressing his name, I sigh. I bring the phone to my ear.

"Rosehaven Rest Home. Rita speaking."

I swallow hard. "Hi Rita. It's Jessie Lane here. Can I speak to my dad, please?"

She's quiet for a moment. "I'm sorry, Jessie. He's not having a good day today."

My throat tightens. Dad has early onset Alzheimer's and is deteriorating faster than the doctors said he would. *Today of all days.*

"Okay. I understand. Please let him know I called and that I love him."

"Of course I will."

I let out a sigh as I disconnect the call.

The minibar beckons and I've got nothing else to do before I fly back to California tomorrow.

I close my eyes.

My stomach rolls.

I don't want to be here.

There's something not right about my agent's offices.

They're in a bad part of town where the buildings all look rundown, and his is no exception.

It's in a big empty parking lot, with a half dozen offices at one end. Maybe they used to be stores—I don't know, but the peeled paint and signs so faded you can't make out what they say.

Split into two groups of three, a dark alley lies between them. I don't even want to know what might go on down there.

Mom pulls into the parking space.

I shudder as I climb out of the car, wrinkling my nose at the unmistakeable smell of urine coming from alley, and, for a moment I consider running away.

But I know I won't get far with no money and no proof of mistreatment. Dad chooses to bury his head in the sand or get beaten down by Mom. No one will take me seriously. What would

I complain about? My mother drove me to an unsavoury part of town?

"Let's go, Jessie." *My mother flashes a brilliant smile at me. She's excited.*

My stomach rolls again.

She taps on Davis's door, and he opens it with a grin.

"Come in."

The overpowering scent of body spray hits me from outside. He's wearing a cheap suit, his greasy dark hair slicked back. I screw up my nose.

Mom steps in first, and I close my eyes briefly before following.

I don't want to be here.

I don't want to be here.

I don't want to be here.

The chant starts in my head.

She pats the couch next to her, and I sink onto the seat.

Davis hovers over us. "I've got some great news, Jessie. You got the commercial."

He smiles, and I shudder. I can't help it. Beside me, my mother claps and hoots like I've won an Oscar.

"Mom."

"We need to celebrate, honey."

Davis nods. "Yes, you do. But first, I'd like to have a chat with Jessie about the job. There are some things I think we need to go over. It'll be pretty boring stuff. I just want to go over lines a few times. So maybe you could find somewhere to go for an hour, Abigail?"

She blanches, but recovers quickly.

Three weeks ago, we sat in this room and she told him that we would do anything to get me into show business. The word anything *has hung over me ever since. Not her. Never her. She throws words around like that, but something tells me I'll be the one paying whatever the price is.*

"Ms. Lane?" he asks, as if reminding her he'd asked a question.

"Of course." Her smile is barely there, but she smiles and my heart sinks. "Anything for Jessie's future."

She stands on shaky legs and makes her way to the door.

As she opens it and steps through, I shoot off the couch and follow her outside.

Mom keeps her head high as she turns and grasps my shoulders. "Go back in there and you do whatever he tells you to do. No matter what."

"But Mom ..."

Her brows knit, and she fixes her steely glare on me. "I know that this commercial is small fry, but Davis is going to get us to where we want to go. And we're going to the top. No one is going to drag us down, Jessie. Not your father. Not you. So you get in there and do whatever you have to in order to keep Davis happy."

My heart thuds. "I don't want to."

The crack of her slap echoes across the empty parking lot. Tears spring up in my eyes, and I try to control my breathing.

But there's no remorse on my mother's face. Instead, she draws in a deep breath. "Do as you're told."

She turns me around and pushes me back toward the door. My feet are like lead as I push it open and Davis ushers me in toward the couch. I screw up my nose as I'm sure the flower pattern on it covers stains. This whole place is gross. Why can't Mom see that?

She doesn't want to.

He closes the door, and the snick of the lock makes me look over my shoulder.

He smiles, and I try desperately to swallow down the acid taste in my throat. His arm wraps around my shoulders. "Such a good girl. Let's get started because we want to make the most of our time together, don't we?"

I down a mini vodka bottle and grimace.

I've never been a big drinker. Years of living with Dad drowning himself in whiskey made sure of that.

But tonight I'm so empty. There's no one I can really call —not that I want sympathy.

Today should have freed me just a little, but even with my mother in the ground, I'm still haunted by memories of her.

I'm not sure enough alcohol exists for this night.

2

JESSIE

My stomach plummets.

For the last week, I've been expecting a final call about the latest role I auditioned for, and now I know why my agent might have been withholding the news.

"What do you mean, 'difficult to work with'?" I tap my red painted nails on the marble countertop of my kitchen. This isn't good. I know I'm not the easiest person all of the time, but I've never missed out on a job because of it.

Until now.

"Well ..." my manager, Marcus, starts.

"Four call-backs, Marcus. They wouldn't have done that if they weren't keen."

"I know, Jess. But I think they took their time because your reputation precedes you and they had trouble making the final decision."

"My reputation?"

He lets out a loud sigh. "We both know you can be a little ... diva-ish."

"Is that even a word?"

"Whether it is or not, you know what it means."

"I really wanted this." Tears prick my eyes. I know I can get a little out of control, but I never thought it'd impact my career. I've seen actors much more famous than I am doing far worse than I've ever done.

Bet this wouldn't be happening if I was a man.

"I know you did. I do have some other news." He pauses. "That role in the Clay Toogood movie you auditioned for what seems like a million years ago?"

For a moment, I wrack my brain, and my heart sinks. "Oh. The *Pretty Woman* rip-off?"

He laughs. "You're not wrong."

"Pole dancer instead of a hooker, but it's pretty damn close." That audition was a year and a half ago, and I had a crash course in pole dancing just in case I got the job. But last I heard, the film had been set back by funding issues.

"Anyway, a new studio has got involved and they want you for the role. I know it's not as big a part as the other one, but it's a decent payday, and you'll be starring opposite Declan O'Leary."

Ugh.

I've met Declan before. He was the Josh Carter of his time, about twenty years ago. Nice guy, but I've heard stories about him turning to the bottle as his career entered a death spiral.

"This is going straight to DVD, isn't it?" I ask.

There's a pause again. "I think so. Their plans for a

theatre release seem a bit up in the air. I can say no if you want me to. I won't push you."

That's the thing I like about Marcus. There are some awful managers out there—like Josh's old manager, Mac. He was with Mac for years. Mac would essentially accept the roles and then tell Josh where he was going. I'm not sure why Josh split from him, but it happened sometime after the movie Josh and I made together.

I'd thought that film was the answer to my prayers at the time. It gave me romantic scenes with Josh and the credibility of playing opposite him.

The movie did just fine at the box office, but I disappeared into the background as the limelight fell on Josh.

Anyone else I'd resent, but I could never do that with either him or Reece. They deserve all the good things to come to them too. I just wish I had an ounce of what they had.

"Jessie?"

"Fine. I'll take it."

"Are you sure?"

When I take a beat to answer, Marcus fills the gap. "How about I wait until tomorrow to let them know. Give you the night to think about it?"

I swallow. "There's not really much to think about. I could do with the job, and who knows? It might end up being a surprise hit. The worst they want from me is to dress in hot pants and a crop top, right?"

He laughs. "That's as far as it goes. I wouldn't even have put you forward for this if I thought it crossed lines."

I let out a breath. Marcus knows my limits and doesn't

push them, and I'm grateful for that. And that's without him knowing about the shitty things that happened in my past. It's why I'm never likely to look for another manager.

"I'll give you a call in the morning to confirm before I call them. Okay?" he asks.

"Sounds good."

"Other than that, there are more irons in the fire, but nothing that's close yet. But as always, I'll keep you posted. You doing okay?"

I swivel on the barstool. "Yeah."

"That's an enthusiastic response. How did your trip to Florida go?"

I run my palm down my face. "The funeral was small. It poured with rain. I buried my mother. It's all done with."

"For what it's worth, I'm sorry."

Snorting, I shake my head. "Don't be. I'm not."

"I'm sorry if I said the wrong thing."

I let out a sigh. "You didn't. It's just ... she was a really shitty mother and I hadn't seen her in years."

"I hope the trip gave you some closure, then."

I swing around and push myself off the stool. "I guess it did in some ways."

"Talk to you tomorrow?"

"You bet."

I blow out a long, loud breath after disconnecting the call.

My life is a mess. I missed out on the role I really wanted, and landed one that's going nowhere. But work is work and it's not the worst thing I've ever been offered.

This isn't fair. I paid such a huge price when I started in

this industry, and I've spent years fighting for what's owed to me. Maybe I push the envelope at times, but I'm always at work on time and do whatever's required, and I know I'm good.

I'm not about to sell myself short.

I push the conversation I just had to the back of my mind and shrug. That part obviously wasn't for me. I'll just have to find something bigger—something better.

Taking a deep breath, I close my eyes.

My mother always said I was destined for the top. But then again, she said a lot of other things that turned out to be untrue.

Thinking of her always makes my faith in myself waver.

A soft tap on the door jolts me out of my thoughts.

Who on earth is visiting me?

No one ever visits.

You need friends to get visitors.

That thought should hit me harder, but I shrug, place the phone back on the charger, and head toward the door.

As I pull my door open, I tilt my head at the sight of Reece Evans, one hand pressed against the wall beside the door, framing himself in the best light possible.

He can be a bit vain.

"Reece." I smile.

This is unexpected. My friendship with Reece has well and truly been on the backburner since he and Delaney's friend, Pania, got together. I've barely heard from him, and now he's on my doorstep.

He scratches the back of his neck. "I'm sorry I didn't call first. I was nearby, and I thought ..."

"It's always good to see you. Come in."

His shoulders slump in relief as I step back and he walks through my door. "It's just been a while. And I feel guilty about not calling you more often."

I nod, not really knowing what to say. "Want a coffee?"

"I'd love one. I'm at a bit of a loose end today, so I'm not in any rush."

Closing the door, I walk into the kitchen. "I just got a Nespresso machine. It's not anywhere near as good as I'm sure Delaney makes, but it's decent."

He laughs. "Sounds good. Should have known you'd be privy to my habit of visiting Delaney for food."

I pop the capsules into the machine. "I've seen that first cooking video, the one you made with her."

There's silence, and I look over my shoulder to see his raised eyebrows. "What? I *am* able to acknowledge her existence."

Those brows knit. "I know, but I try to avoid bringing her up because I know there's no love lost between you."

"I don't hate her. It just hurt to realise Josh chose her. Although, I think I always knew that would be the case." I grab the cups and pour the coffee. Reece doesn't care how the coffee comes, so I make it the same as my own, adding a spoon of *Splenda* before walking back into the living room and handing him the cup.

He sits on the couch, and I sit opposite, pulling my bare feet under me on the recliner.

"So. Catch me up on all things Jessie. How's it going?" he asks, and takes a sip of coffee. "That hits the spot."

"I'm sure your life is way more interesting."

He shakes his head. "I've got news but I want to hear how things are in your world. What's new?"

"I missed out on a job because I'm difficult to work with." I lean back and roll my eyes.

Reece doesn't react.

I sit up straight. "Don't you think that's unfair?" All I want is someone on my side. That person has always been Reece.

"Don't hate me." He takes another sip, and my anxiety rises as he takes his time continuing. "But I'm kinda surprised it's taken this long."

I huff. "I'm not that bad."

Reece purses his lips as he seems to be thinking about what to say next. "You can be very ... demanding."

My stomach sinks. "I don't mean to be."

"Maybe not, but ..." He sighs. "Look, Jess. You're a star. You're beautiful, you're insanely talented, and ..." Reece pauses and I place my cup on a side table and bury my face in my hands. "Sometimes you just let it go to your head."

"Put me in one of your movies then." I drop my hands.

He leans his head back on the couch and rolls it from side to side. "I can't. You'll need to make things up with Josh for that to happen. Things would be so much easier if you just sorted things out with Delaney."

I cover my face with my hand. "I'm not sure how."

"Just go and talk to her. She's not a terrible person." He puts down his coffee cup. "I had something happen to me a while ago that I reacted badly to, and it took people who care about me to hammer it home that I needed to get myself together. I'm trying to be that person to you."

My eyebrows rise. "What happened to you?"

His lips curl into a smile. "I found out I had a long-lost brother."

I let my mouth fall open. "No."

"Yes. Alex Stone is my half-brother. We share a father."

I can't breathe. It wasn't that long ago that Reece told me about his parents dying and how he was raised by his grandmother. Now this man I've known for the past ten years suddenly has more family? "Oh, Reece. That's amazing."

"Yeah, I didn't take it well at first." He shrugs. "But Pania, Josh, and Alex's wife talked me around. And it's a good thing." Reece grins. "It's not just a brother. I have a niece now."

"Instant family."

"Something like that." He reaches over and gives my knee a squeeze. "Sort things out with Delaney and you'll be part of our extended family too."

I shrug. "I'm not sure if Josh will ever really forgive me."

"He's a good guy. And you know that. It's why you love him."

I gulp. "I'm over that. I should have realised a long time ago that I would never be the one for him. I'm glad he's happy. I'm glad *you're* happy."

His face contorts into something I've never seen before. He looks almost dazed, and I don't have to ask to know he's thinking about his girlfriend.

"Didn't think it was possible. It's like everything just slotted into place, you know?" He meets my gaze. "My friendship with Josh kept me from drifting, but now I have foundations."

Tears prick my eyes. "I love that for you."

His lips twitch into a smile. "I know there are things you don't talk about from your past. That was me too. But, Jessie, opening up is the best thing I ever did. You know I'm always here to listen."

I chew my bottom lip. Maybe Reece is right. But I couldn't bear it if I told him my whole story and he looked at me with pity or disgust. I'm not prepared to take the risk—especially when Reece is probably the last of my good friends.

Even if I did confide in him, I know he's never going to hang out with me the way he used to now he has Pania in his life. I don't resent her, but there's a part of me that knows I'm missing out.

I've never had a problem with confrontation, but something about apologising to Delaney scares me. What if she rejects my apology? What if I make things worse? I'm not sure I can look her in the eye after the things I said. I made a scene in her own diner and called her a whore.

Even after she'd shown me some kindness.

"Maybe one day, Reece."

He frowns. "All you need to do is call. Things might have changed in my life, but I'll always be your friend."

"Does Pania know you're here?"

His eyes widen like he's been caught out. "No. It really was a spur-of-the-moment thing. But I'll tell her. She's not a terrible person."

"You wouldn't love her if she was. I don't think she's terrible, but she's terrifying."

He chuckles. "Yes, yes she is. It's one of the things I love most about her." After picking up his coffee cup, he drains it and stands. "I should get going. Got any more work in the pipeline?"

I sigh. "Yeah. Some probably straight-to-video B-movie rip-off of *Pretty Woman*."

He grimaces. "Ouch."

"It's not the worst thing I've ever done. Maybe it'll be a surprise hit."

He turns toward the kitchen, strides into it, and rinses out his cup, placing it beside the sink. "I wish I could do more."

"It's not on you." I stand, tucking my hands into my jeans pockets. "I got myself into this spot, and I'll just have to work myself out of it."

Reece walks back toward me and chucks me under the chin. "That's my girl. You have to keep thinking positive. And keep in touch because you never know what might come up."

"Thanks, Reece."

"See you soon." He pecks me on the cheek. "And think about that whole 'making amends with Delaney' thing because if that gets sorted out, then you get to spend more time with the magic that is me."

I laugh, slapping his arm. "You're such a dick."

"I know, but that's what makes me loveable." He grins.

"It's true." I hold up my hands and he laughs.

"Catch you later, Jess."

When he's gone, I sit back on the couch and draw in a deep breath.

I've made good money from my career. Maybe I haven't achieved everything I wanted, but I'm in a position with my savings where I don't really have to work. Mama Lane might have been a crappy mother, but the one thing she did right was teach me how to live frugally.

I've saved every penny I could since I started acting, and it's been enough to set me up for life, but I don't want to rest on my laurels. I want more.

Josh went out and bought a huge house with the first big pay check he got. I bought a tiny apartment because I didn't need the space, and any extravagant purchases have been maintaining my image, like clothing and shoes.

My apartment's filled with mementos and reminders of my journey.

But it's not enough.

And I don't even know if getting all the roles I want would be enough.

My best friends are either deeply involved with their own families or not talking to me anymore. I don't know how to reach out.

They say pride comes before a fall, and I blush at how much I've let mine take over.

The man I loved was lost to me a long time ago. Josh is with Delaney for life.

Reece is still my friend but so distant that he may as well not be.

Now my career has been impacted by my pride.

And I'm lonely.

What do I do?

3

SHANE

There's nothing like a beer after a long day.

And today's been the pits.

A power failure this morning followed by the generator not starting caused delays with milking the cows. And then there was the errant sheep which managed to escape and take us all on a merry dance around the yard before we managed to get hold of it.

I take a long drag of my beer and close my eyes when my mobile rings.

Marcus.

We met through an old army buddy of mine who's now living in New Mexico, and we took an instant liking to each other. When he heard I worked in security, he hired me to take care of one of his clients a couple of years ago when he had trouble with a persistent fan. Since then I've done a few smaller jobs for him, but I decided a while ago not to do any more. I hate traveling, and it takes time away from the job I do now—running this farm with my friends.

Frowning at my phone, I press the *accept call* button. Might as well listen before I say no.

"Marcus."

"Shane. It's been a while." His extra warm tone makes me roll my eyes. Marcus can be a smooth talker when he wants to be—I guess it goes with the job. Last time we spoke, I told him I wasn't interested in any more work from him. Must be a big favour he needs. "I need your expertise."

"There's no one closer?"

"After what you did for Weston, I'd rather have you than anyone else on the job."

I've heard that before. Weston Pryor, teen star, had a girl persistently breaking his security at the estate he'd bought from selling about a billion albums. When Marcus asked me to oversee his security, I found a right royal mess and burned it all to the ground before setting up a whole new system.

His harasser was soon caught and finally faced charges.

"I've got an actor client who's being threatened. And the threats are getting worse and worse. It … uhh … took a while to put it all together, so we're behind the eight ball on this. I need her safe, and I need you here as soon as possible."

I blow out a breath. "Let me guess. Some spoiled Hollywood princess who pissed off the wrong person?"

Marcus is quiet, and I just know I've hit the nail on the head.

"Jessie can be a bit … highly strung. But she's done nothing to cause this level of reaction."

I swivel my gaze around the room. Cookie's standing at

the kitchen bench, leaning on his elbows, clearly listening in on my conversation. I flip him the bird, and he grins.

"Wasn't suggesting that she had. Someone's clearly taking it too far, but can you think of anyone she might have pissed off?"

"The list is probably pretty long by now. And I have people working on that. What I need is someone I can trust to act as her bodyguard until we work it out."

I rub my face with my palm. "I really thought you'd opt for someone closer. I told you last time I was done."

He huffs. "There's no one I trust more. And this is a special case. Jessie's very important to me."

Right.

"I see." I chuckle to myself.

"Stop it," he growls. "I'm nearly old enough to be her father. There's just ... A little over ten years ago, I met this scrawny teenager with a haunted look in her eyes, and she just blew me away with how talented she was. Something put that look there. She might have learned how to mask it, but she's got her demons, and I decided in that moment I'd always be in her corner no matter what. She's a real challenge as a client, but damn, Shane, she's the most talented actress I've seen in my career."

His words bring a smile to my lips. It takes a lot to impress Marcus, and he handles some of the biggest stars in Hollywood. I'm not a big movie watcher, so I wouldn't have a clue who's who.

Marcus is asking for me because he knows he can trust me to do the best job I can.

Plus, the pay is good. And the kind of working relationship we have is worth more than the money.

And the farm does need to top up the coffers after finishing the expansion we just built.

"Shane. I'm sorry to push you, but I need an answer."

I look back at Cookie. His arms are crossed, and he's got one eyebrow raised. I'm sure he's worked out by now I'm being offered a job, and the only question he's going to ask me when the call ends is *'How much?'*

"Yes. Of course I'm up for it. You know you can always count on me."

He breathes a sigh of relief. "Thanks. I'll get my assistant to book your flight for as soon as possible and send you the details."

"That'd be great."

"Now I just have to convince Jessie this is a good idea. Great to talk to you."

He disconnects the call before I can respond.

What?

He hasn't told her that she's getting a bodyguard yet?

I can't help but think that he's putting the cart before the horse, but then he's paying for that privilege.

Pressing my head against the back of the couch, I close my eyes briefly. I said my last trip would be the final one, but the money's just too good to turn down.

"How much?" Cookie asks.

I pick up a cushion from the couch and throw it at him. "You're so predictable."

He laughs as he catches it. "I didn't hear all of it, but I'm guessing it pays well."

"*Very* well. Marcus always pays the big dollars for results. This'll be enough to cover the expansion."

Cookie whistles. "Wow. Best get on that plane then."

There's a thud as Ajax makes his way through the back door and into the kitchen. Doesn't matter how long we've all lived here, or how many times he comes through that door, every time, he hits that doorframe.

I smile to myself.

"Plane?" Ajax asks.

I thought I was a big guy until I met Ajax. While I'm six foot six, he's closer to seven foot. He's also surprisingly agile for his size—makes me feel like a big oaf. And out of all of us, he's the one who's in tune with and incredibly gentle to the farm animals.

Originally, the plan was to grow the herd and make a go of dairy farming. But with Cookie's talents in the kitchen, we soon realised we were better off diversifying and branching out into artisanal products.

The expansion was mainly in the field of cheese production, but we also invested in new smokers for the bacon. Most of the cost was the construction to make the work sheds bigger, but Cookie's confident there won't be any waste of space.

"What plane?" Ajax asks again. "I thought you were done with that shit."

"Well, I was."

My phone dings with an incoming email. I pull it up and my eyes widen at the amount he's offering. This really is big, even for Marcus.

"Good news?" Cookie asks.

"You could say that. This will more than cover our expansion."

"That good, huh?" Ajax's brows rise.

"That good."

"Sounds to me like you'd better get on that plane, then."

"Go and pack. Where are you going?" Cookie chin-lifts toward me.

"LA." I chuckle as I head to my room. Marcus wants me there as fast as possible. Can't say I'm looking forward to it, but at the same time, it'll be good to break up the monotony of farm life.

Los Angeles, here I come.

4

JESSIE

I hate my life.

When I took this job, I knew this movie wasn't going to set the world on fire. But I've worked on worse, and there's no way I'm going to bring anything less than my A game.

But I've already fought with wardrobe over the outfits I agreed to versus what they tried to get me to wear.

I've been there, done that before.

And if I'm going to get my breasts out, it'd better be for the big screen.

I'm not needed on set for about twenty minutes, so I head from wardrobe to my trailer wrapped in a big fluffy robe. I'm not walking around with my ass hanging out when I don't need to.

I tug open the door and step in.

It's not the greatest trailer in the world, but it's clean and tidy. That's all I need. I've known some actors to rant and make demands about their trailers, and while I've developed this reputation for being difficult, I've never complained about anything so trivial.

There's a shoebox on the table.

It's not uncommon to get given gifts on set. Security usually check them over before they make it to the trailer

This doesn't have a card with it, just my name written in bright red Sharpie on the top.

I smile, removing the lid.

There's a mess of tissue paper and I tug at it until it parts.

Blinking rapidly, my heart thuds as I'm greeted by a rat's body. There's no head. Bright red blood is smeared around the edges of the box, showing just how fresh it is.

Is this a sick joke?

I back away, open the door of the trailer, and let out a scream for help. A security guard runs from somewhere by the set and I shake as I step down and out of the trailer.

"Ms Lane?"

"There's ... there's a dead rat in my trailer."

He takes hold of my trembling hands. I flinch. It should be comforting, but it's not, and a knot of anxiety starts forming in my stomach.

I pull my hands away.

"Stay here," he says.

I nod rapidly, raising my gaze to a small crowd of extras gathering nearby. No one approaches to check on me. I shouldn't be surprised. This is what I've done—created a reputation for being a diva to the point where now something like this has happened, and it's just a curiosity.

No one actually cares.

Behind me, the security guard calls someone on his radio, and I steady my breath, sucking in the fresh air and closing my eyes.

Before I know it, another security guard is steering me toward the set.

"We'll take care of this, Ms Lane. I know you're due on set shortly, so it might be best to wait things out there."

He guides me inside to a long row of chairs. I drop into the one with my name on it.

"Thank you," I say.

"Want me to stay with you?"

I shake my head. "I'm sure your talents are needed at my trailer."

He nods. "Of course."

I blow out a long breath.

There's no way I can let this shoot get out of control. If I'm scraping the bottom of the barrel making this movie and I screw it up, then I'll be making these types of movies for the rest of my career—or worse.

"Jessie." Clay walks toward me with a smile on his face. "Ready to make some movie magic?"

I force a smile. Should I tell Clay about the situation in my trailer? In the past, I might have made a big deal about it, but for the sake of my career, I still need to keep a lid on my feelings.

No. I'll just get through this and get home for the day. "Sure am."

"We're nearly ready for you."

Movie magic is slow to make.

I've worked hard on my craft. I'm not known for messing up lines or missing my mark, but take after take, I fail spectacularly.

This role is already scraping the bottom of the barrel, but somehow, I'm managing to make things even worse.

Clay starts off all smiles and patience, but when I screw up one more time, he calls time out and walks toward me, frustration written all over his face. "What's going on, Jessie?"

I drop my arms to my sides. "I'm sorry. I'm really having trouble focusing."

"No shit." He pinches the bridge of his nose.

"It's just ..." I bite my lip. "I found something in my trailer that really bothered me, and I don't want to make a fuss."

"I see." His tone is flat, and he taps his foot against the linoleum floor impatiently. "I don't have time for any dramas, Jessie."

"It was a decapitated rat in a box."

Clay gently takes hold of my arm. "What did you say?"

"Clearly someone doesn't like me. It was right before I came out to do the scene, and I didn't want to cause delays because I really need this job." I gulp. "I didn't want to make anyone think I was acting like a diva."

He drops his hands to his sides. "I'm sorry if I made you feel—"

"No, it's fine. I also didn't really have much time to process it."

Clay studies me for a moment. "I'll check in with security on it. No one should have been able to leave anything in your trailer."

"I'd appreciate that." I clasp my hands together. "I want to do the scene again."

He shakes his head. "We'll pick up in the morning if we have to."

"I'm not working tomorrow so I don't want to. Security are looking into it, and I've already held everyone up enough." I draw in a deep breath. There's no way I'm letting this screw this up for me. "Let's nail this sucker."

And that's exactly what I do.

ONCE THE SCENE IS DONE, I walk back toward my trailer. Two police officers are standing outside it, and one greets me with a cautious smile.

I thought the worst part of the day was filming the first scene of the movie. For me, that's the toughest part of starting a film. But the thought of having to speak with the police is on a whole other level.

"We still have to fingerprint the trailer, Miss Lane. I'm sorry; you can't go in there."

My shoulders slump. "Can I at least get my things?"

"What things do you need?"

Puffing out a breath, I cross my arms. "My car keys, my purse, and my phone. They're all in my bag in my trailer."

"You don't have a driver?"

"No. My car's in the parking lot. If I can't use my trailer before I leave then I want to just get out of here." I tap my foot on the gravel. "Please. There's a large black bag in there with my things in it. That's all I want."

One of the officers opens the trailer door and speaks to someone inside before passing out my bag.

I breathe a sigh of relief just to have that tiny piece of normalcy when my day has been anything but.

Grabbing my phone out of my bag, I steady my trembling hands and dial Marcus. Someone may have already called him, but I need to make sure he knows what's happened if they haven't.

"Jessie." Marcus always greets me warmly, and I need that so badly right now.

"Marcus. Something happened on set. Someone left a dead rat in my trailer missing its head. It was boxed up like a gift." The words tumble out of me at a million miles an hour.

"Take a deep breath. There was *what?*" Marcus practically yells down the phone. "Sorry. I'm not angry at you. Obviously. How the fuck did that happen?"

"I'm not sure. Site security called the police in, and I can't get back into my trailer today. I don't know where to go from here."

"I know you don't have any scenes tomorrow. Come in and see me. There's something I need to discuss with you anyway."

I bite my lip. "Sure."

By the time I've finished talking to him, I'm feeling a lot better.

At least I have Marcus in my corner.

He seemed cagey about whatever it was he needs to talk to me about. I hope it's a new role, but today's events have me unsettled.

Tomorrow has to be better.

5

JESSIE

Something's going on and I don't like it.

First, the issue in my trailer and now Marcus wants me to go to his office to meet with him. He hasn't asked me to do that in forever.

Last time, it was because I'd secured what I thought at the time was my dream role. He'd wanted to celebrate.

But there's nothing I'm waiting on, and unless some miracle has occurred and I've got someone pursuing me for a role, I'm at a loss to know what the meeting will be about.

It wasn't that long ago I begrudgingly accepted this role. Now, I really hope I haven't lost it. While I controlled my reaction to yesterday's events as best I could, there was a lot of time wasted yesterday because of me.

My heels clack on the tiled floor as I make my way to the receptionist. She looks up and smiles widely. "Ms Lane."

"Hi, Marilyn. I have an appointment with Marcus at ten?"

She picks up the phone. "I'll let him know you're here."

It only takes a moment and she smiles again. "Go right in."

I walk past her desk and down the corridor that leads to his office. Marcus's business is thriving. As well as me, he manages some of the biggest stars in Hollywood. He could have passed me off to one of his associates when my job offers were clearly declining, but he didn't, and for that I'm grateful.

After tapping on his door, I turn the handle and walk in.

It's like coming home.

As he's the head of the agency, his office is huge. When I first came here, the large, warmly furnished room was intimidating. It was a far cry from the stained couch in Davis's hovel. I knew then I'd lucked out with management.

Marcus's company does so well, he could afford newer, more opulent offices than these, but I think he likes people feeling at home, and the large sprawling couches here are the best to sink into.

He stands and walks around his desk.

"Jessie." He opens his arms and I walk straight into them. Marcus has been my manager since I was nineteen. He's known about all my ups and downs these past ten years, and always tried his best to support me, even though I'm sure I've been very trying at times.

He's the father I wish I had.

As he lets me go, he runs his hands down my arms and takes my hands in his. "How are you doing?"

I pull away and shrug, dropping onto his office sofa. "I was okay until yesterday."

He sits on a sofa opposite me. "Is that really true?"

"I'm making a movie I'm not really that excited about and then this happened. I'm just wondering what's next." I puff out a breath, blowing a stray lock of hair out of my face.

His lips tighten. "That's what I wanted to talk to you about today. Yesterday's issue in your trailer. It's an escalation."

I blink rapidly. "An escalation?"

He drops his gaze. "About a week ago, one of the mail clerks brought a note to my attention. It was a rambling diatribe about you and a threat."

I gasp. "A threat?"

He nods slowly. "She's quite new and hadn't come across anything like it before. But we get all kinds of mail for clients, so it's not necessarily unusual, and you know we had a group of Josh Carter fans get upset simply because you acted opposite him."

My stomach rolls. I know about those letters. There'd been plenty of comments on social media too. Josh has some ardent fans who throw hate around like confetti if they don't like you being matched with him romantically in a movie. There were no threats, but plenty of name calling.

"So, she shared it with a co-worker, and ... I've had my staff go through all the mail we've received for you in the past few months. No one picked up a pattern until now."

"What do you mean?"

He fists his hands, squeezing tight and then releasing. He does this when he's nervous about telling me bad news. At least I recognise it.

"There's a pattern. You've been sent warnings for a while from someone with a grudge."

I blink rapidly. "A grudge?"

"Jessie, I'm so sorry. We should have seen it and dealt with it, but the system we have apparently doesn't work when multiple people open the mail and no one's overseeing it. The other clerk had seen something similar so reported it to their supervisor. We have threats going back months demanding that you give up your career."

My stomach plummets.

"I've reported the whole thing to the police along with the rat in your trailer. The handwriting matches—the threats are from the same person. There's a detective assigned to the case, and they'll want to talk to you, but I wanted to explain and apologise first."

"Why would anyone want to hurt me?"

The worst thing about this is that I could name a hundred people I've pissed off over the years. There could be a hundred different answers to my question.

"This is different. Someone bypassed security to leave you a message in your trailer. They crossed a line in sending you one threatening letter, but after six, they've clearly decided to take matters into their own hands."

Cupping my face in my hands, I don't even have it in me to cry.

"I'm bringing in personal security. Someone low-key who can shadow you and make sure you're safe."

I look up and puff out an exasperated breath. "I'm sure that's not necessary."

His pale blue eyes pull me in with their sincerity, and he grips my arm. "Trust me. It is." He looks over my shoulder and calls out, "Come in, Shane."

I turn as a giant appears in the door.

A dark-haired, bearded giant.

I run my gaze up all six-foot-whatever-he-is. The man's unmissable. "*This* is someone low-key?"

The giant standing in front of me smirks. "No one's ever called me low-key." His voice is so deep, I swear the floor rumbles below me.

It's also insanely hot.

No. There's no way you're going there.

"Are you sure this is really necessary?" I turn back toward Marcus. "Can't I just ... I don't know ... be more careful?"

He nods. "Jessie, someone wants to hurt you. The threats are serious. I'm going to pull out all the stops to keep you safe."

"And this Neanderthal is supposed to be all the stops?" I turn and shoot a smile at the tall guy. "No offence."

"None taken," he responds. "This Neanderthal is pretty good at his job."

My mouth falls open, and I stop myself from saying anything further. I know I shouldn't have said it, but no one ever throws my words in my face. It's unsettling.

Marcus flicks his gaze between us. "I wouldn't do this if I wasn't worried."

I let out a loud sigh and shake off his hands. "Fine. Whatever. I just want to get back to work."

"About that ..."

Tension grips my chest. "Please don't tell me I have to step down from the movie."

His eyes widen. "Shit. No. I don't mean anything bad. It's just that the producers have offered to shift the shooting schedule a little to give you a few days to get yourself together if you need it."

My eyebrows rise. "Really?"

"Truth is, they've already shot too much of the film to get rid of you. Not that there was ever any talk about that. They love you."

Relief floods my system. "I should hope so, given how much ass-shaking I've already done."

A deep snicker behind me brings a smile to my face, and Marcus laughs. "I've heard they're very impressed with your pole work."

I chuckle. "I've never had stronger abs."

"I'm very pleased you're laughing, Jessie. I worry about you sometimes."

I wave him away. "You don't have to worry about me. I'm a bundle of joy."

He gets up and walks over to the couch, dropping onto it beside me and wiping away a tear I didn't even feel from my cheek. "I know this is a lot to take in. So please, accept this help until we track down this sick asshole."

I nod. Marcus has stood by me through good and bad. Maybe I don't have a ton of friends, but I know I can count on him. Instead of cutting ties with me, he's kept on trying to get me jobs.

So even though the tall, dark, and delicious man

standing behind us isn't something I planned for, I'll do whatever Marcus asks me to do.

"How bad were these threats?" I ask.

"Bad enough for me to get you the best man I know for security. Shane's looked after my clients before, and I trust him with my life."

I flick a glance at the big guy. "Okay."

"He's going to have to stay with you for a while. You all good with that, or do you need me to find you a hotel?"

"Home will be fine. There's security at the door and you can't get in without a code. I've always felt safe there."

He looks up at Shane, who nods.

"I'll check it out," Shane says.

"Whatever." I examine my fingernails, catching him raising an eyebrow out the corner of my eye.

"Jessie," Marcus says.

I look up to meet Marcus's gaze. "What?"

"This is for your own good. Stop being a brat."

I shrug and look away. My life is far from perfect, but it's mine. I hate the idea of someone tailing me, even if it's for my own safety. Not to mention having to share my personal space with someone I don't know. "I hate this."

He reaches for my hands. "I know you do. So do I. Let us do our jobs, keep you safe, and get to the bottom of this. Okay, kiddo?"

"Okay."

"Now, get out of here and enjoy your days off."

He pecks me on the cheek, and I stand, looking toward Shane. "Come on, babysitter. Let's go."

Shane chuckles as I walk around the couch and toward the door.

I'm not sure how serious these threats are, but whoever has made them has made it clear they can get to me. I have no doubt Shane's presence will make me feel safe, but at what personal cost?

What a mess.

6

___

SHANE

essie Lane is gorgeous.

She's around five-foot-eight and has the body of a cover model, with long auburn hair and green eyes.

She has attitude, and she owns it.

I follow her out of Marcus's office, observing her the whole way. She holds her spine straight, her shoulders back, and her nose in the air as if everyone else is below her.

They probably are.

The only reason she can't get away with doing that to me is because I'm that much taller than her. Confidence exudes from her pores as she stalks down the street and toward her car.

"You don't have a driver?" I ask.

"Only when I'm out of town." She presses the key fob and a Volkswagen Golf lights up.

Shit.

"And *that's* your car?"

Her gaze flicking between me and the car, she turns her head, drops her sunglasses down her nose, and lets out a giggle before coming to a stop. She holds up the keys with her other hand. "I'm guessing you're going to drive."

"Well, yeah. If I can fit in the damn thing."

After throwing my bag in the back, I open the driver's door.

She doesn't move. Instead, she takes out her phone and starts snapping photos.

"What are you doing?"

She drops her hands to her sides. "Waiting for you to get into the car so I can take photos. I think you're bigger than the front seat."

I frown, drop into the front seat, and push it back as far as I can.

Jessie laughs. And it's not the dainty laugh I thought would come out of her—it's a from-the-gut belly laugh.

She's got her phone back up and she's clicking away.

"Get in the car, Jessie," I say.

After throwing her phone in her bag, she holds up her hands. "Okay. Whatever you say, Mr Neanderthal."

She clasps them together and makes her way to the passenger side, then slides into the seat.

When I asked Marcus if this case would involve working with some spoiled Hollywood princess, I didn't really expect to be right. In the past, I've met actors and found them quite reasonable as a whole. I think I've got my work cut out with this one.

"I'm sorry," she says. "The last twenty-four hours have been really stressful, and now I find I've gained a roommate right along with these threats I didn't know about. I really needed to find something to laugh about."

Shit.

I didn't think of that. She's just had all this information dumped on her as well as dealing with yesterday's little gift in her trailer. I'm sure her head's all over the place.

"Happy you find my squeezing into your car amusing." I say with a smile. "Now, where am I going?"

She lowers her gaze, then looks at me from under her eyelashes. "My apartment."

"And that is where?"

Jessie lets out another laugh. "Can't I just drive? It's my car."

"You could, but then I'd have to get back out and then in again, and you are *not* taking more photos of me."

She clutches her stomach and laughs again. "You are no fun."

"This isn't a 'fun' situation."

With a roll of her eyes, she cocks her head and waves to the right. "Pull out and go in that direction. I'll show you where to go." She barks out a laugh. "Though I feel like I should be telling you where to go."

Turning the key in the ignition, I get the car started. "I'm here to do a job. That's it. I've seen what's happened so far; someone's got a real hard-on over taking you down."

She swallows hard. "I really am grateful. It's just a lot to take in. I don't mean to take it out on you."

I nod. "I know. Let's get you back home. I assume that's where you feel safe?"

"I do."

"We'll take it from there. Okay?"

She's quiet the rest of the way, pointing out where to go and giving instructions so soft I nearly miss a couple of turns. I don't want to knock the wind out of her system, but she has to take this seriously.

Once again, I'm surprised.

She indicates for me to pull into an underground carpark, and I follow her directions until we come to a stop.

I'm not much of a movie-watching man, but even I've heard of Jessie Lane.

I thought we'd be headed to a big place in the Hollywood Hills. Instead, she lives in a pretty bland-looking apartment block.

The car surprised me too. I've worked security for some of Marcus's clients who travel with drivers everywhere. For all her airs and graces, Jessie driving herself around in this tiny clown car seems uncharacteristic.

I guess she's just full of surprises.

Grabbing my bag, I climb out of the car and lock it up after she steps out.

Jessie leads me to a nearby door and enters a code to open it and we make our way through to the elevator.

"Is that how you get into the building? A code?"

She nods, pressing the elevator button. "Yeah. It's unique to my apartment."

"You the only one with it?"

Pulling her glasses off, she meets my gaze just as the elevator dings. The doors open, and we step inside.

"A couple of my close friends have it. Only one of them ever visits me, and he doesn't come to see me very often." She presses the button for level five.

"Are they trustworthy? These friends?"

Her brows twitch. "Very. I've known them for years, and they wouldn't give the code to anyone or misuse it."

I nod. "Okay. Well, I'm going to talk to building management and have it changed anyway."

"Does it have to?"

The elevator dings, and we step out into a beige corridor. I follow her to the end of it, and we reach her door. "It's the fastest way to make sure it's secure. Other than those friends, does anyone have the code?"

Jessie reaches into her bag and pulls out a set of keys. "Marcus has it. He's my emergency contact."

She slides the key into the lock and pushes open the door.

Following her inside, I take in an apartment which doesn't seem to say, *'A Hollywood star lives here.'* The walls are a burgundy colour, and she's got no artwork or photos gracing them. A cream couch with matching recliners sits in a living room with a large television. On the other side of the room is a small kitchen with a bench.

It's the type of place I used to live in before we bought the farm.

Small. Lonely.

What if Jessie's lonely too?

It makes me wonder if that shell of defensiveness Jessie

has is because of this. She mentioned only one friend visits her and he doesn't do it often. Apart from Marcus, who else does she have?

My jaw clenches at the thought.

She needs me on her side.

And she has me for as long as this thing takes.

Even if she wants to push me away.

7

JESSIE

Shane's quiet, his jaw clenched as he studies the room like he's deep in thought.

"And the rest of the apartment?" He meets my gaze.

I wave my hand around. "Be my guest and look around. There's just the two bedrooms and a single bathroom. Laundry's downstairs."

"Fire escape?"

I nod toward the door. "Out there at the end of the hallway."

He walks toward the first bedroom, and I drop onto the couch as he makes his way back out and into the bathroom. Once he's checked my bedroom, he comes back. "I can work with this."

"So what does being my security entail?" I ask.

"I'll be staying here with you, taking you to and from work—basically shadowing you everywhere you go."

The weight of the past day hits again, and I blink back tears. If these threats had been dealt with earlier, I wouldn't be in this position. *They were in my trailer.*

"Jessie, this person is sick and Marcus isn't about to take any risks as far as you're concerned. I'll keep you safe."

"Promise?" My voice is shaky.

He crosses the room, drops to his knees in front of me, and grasps both my arms to steady me. I breathe slow to hold in the urge to rip my arms away. "Promise."

The sudden rush of tears takes me by surprise, but Shane stays in place, his hands on my forearms, and just his presence gives me reassurance.

"Hey," he says softly. "I'm going to guess you bottle up everything and these tears aren't how you usually react?"

I smile through my tears. "You guessed right."

"I'm the same." He drops his hands. "You're safe with me."

Part of me wants to fling my arms around his impossibly wide shoulders, but I don't know if I could even reach them, and besides, it's probably not really appropriate. I don't know the guy, but I do feel secure in his presence.

"So, what are your plans for the rest of the week if you're not working?"

I shrug. "Sit at home. Learn my lines. Binge watch some Netflix."

He offers me a crooked smile. "I'm down with that."

"No Netflix and chill, though. Sorry. I'm not that kind of girl." I flutter my tear-laden eyelashes at him.

He chuckles. "I'll try and stay out of your way."

"There's no chance of that happening in an apartment

this size." I tilt my head. "Might as well just buy a huge bag of popcorn and camp out in the living room. There's a convenience store two buildings down."

"I've got to go and talk to building management anyway, so I'll pop out and grab some popcorn. I need you to stay here. Don't open the door to anyone."

I suck on my bottom lip, still trying not to cry. After recent events, my head is spinning.

"Where are your keys?"

After reaching into my bag, I pull them out and hand them to him.

"I won't be long. Okay?"

Nodding, I lean back on the couch. "I'll make a head start on that Netflix."

He tilts his head and smiles. "You do that. For the record, I like action movies."

I roll my eyes. "How surprising."

"Actually, I don't have a preference. I'm not much of a movie person. Put on whatever you want."

"As if I wasn't doing that anyway."

Shane chuckles. "How surprising. I'll be back soon."

I fidget the whole time he's gone. Who would want to hurt me? I've clawed my way through situations at times and not been mindful of other people's feelings even when they've done nothing to deserve it. But this?

It has to be someone I've worked with in the past—that much is obvious. But who?

The scrape of a key in the lock makes me jump.

"It's just me," Shane calls out.

He frowns as he walks in the door.

"There aren't any security cameras in this building."

My eyebrows rise. "None?" I can't even remember asking about them when I moved in. The price was right. That was all I cared about.

"We need to relocate you to a hotel."

"No." I cross my arms. "I'm staying right here."

His nostrils flare and he narrows his eyes. "I'll call Marcus."

"You do that." I stare him down until he pulls out a phone and dials Marcus, his gaze fixed on me the whole time.

"Marcus. Shane. This apartment block has no security video. Jessie's turned down my kind invitation to move her to a hotel."

His eyes narrow as Marcus replies, and I pretend to look at my nails again. I've no idea who Marcus will back, but I don't want to move from my home where I'm most comfortable and feel safest.

"You owe me extra for this." He huffs. "Fine. But if something happens, there's no security footage. The security code has been changed. That'll have to do for now."

When he hangs up the call, I cock my head. "Everything okay?"

"Yeah, apart from this stubborn client who's already shown she's going to be a nightmare to work with."

I hold up my palms. "Guilty as charged. And probably why someone wants to hurt me."

"I'm going to tell you one more time. We should move to a hotel."

"What did Marcus say?"

His eyes dart away as if he's trying not to look at me. "He

said I had to balance my concerns with what makes you happy."

I clap my hands together, knowing how annoying I must be. "That's my Marcus."

"What Jessie wants, Jessie gets." His expression looks set in stone, it's so hard. And it makes my heart sink a little to see it.

I caused that.

I didn't need to.

"Basically. Now, popcorn or pizza?" I project the biggest smile I can.

SHANE DISAPPEARS downstairs when the pizza arrives, and I catch my breath.

What he's saying is sensible, but my world's been turned upside down these past few days and all I want to do is curl up on my own damn couch and watch some television.

I'm scared, and I need comfort. Not that I'll ever admit that to anyone.

He walks back in the door with three large pizza boxes, and my mouth waters at the scent of pepperoni in the air.

"Did we really need all this pizza?" he asks.

I let out a giggle. He's such a big guy but only one of those pizzas is his. I eat when I'm stressed, and right now, I've got stress in spades. Pizza isn't something I indulge in when I'm shooting—especially with the skimpy outfits I'm wearing. But I'm wrung out and not going back to set for a few days, so I'm going to eat.

With my day off tomorrow, I'll get in a workout and make up for it. When I auditioned for this movie, I changed up my workout to include pole dancing, and there's an advanced class tomorrow.

"What's that look about?" Shane spreads out the pizza boxes on the coffee table and drops onto the couch beside me.

"What look?"

"The one that tells me you're about to cause trouble."

I shrug. "No idea what you're talking about. Let's eat."

Opening a pizza box, I wolf down three slices of pizza without pause. Shane sits and watches, a slice in his hand and a smirk on his face.

"What?" I ask.

"I'm not sure you even took a breath between each slice. Never seen a woman eat like that before." He chuckles.

"Is that good or bad?"

His eyes widen. "Oh, I'm not commenting on it in that way. It's just, you're such a small thing and I don't know where that pizza disappeared to."

I laugh. "After the day I've had, I was starving."

He nods slowly. "That'd do it." His lips twitch as if he's trying to work out whether to say something or not.

"What?"

"Is it just security you need, or do you need a babysitter? You know, to make sure you eat properly too."

I lean back on the couch and sigh. "Oh, that would be wonderful. I'm so terrible at looking after myself."

He laughs. "Pretty sure I can throw that service in for free."

"No. Please don't. I'll get used to it and when this is all over, I'll miss it too much." I can't help it. I'm starting to like this guy. Even if I'm not that keen on him being here. But there's a reason for his presence and if I linger in my thoughts about it too long, it'll just upset me.

"Hey, hey, hey," Shane says, nudging my arm. "You okay?"

I shudder. "I just need to stop thinking about why you're here."

"It can't be easy."

"It's all very sudden." I close my eyes. "I mean, yesterday, I had no idea about any of this. I found a dead rat in my trailer, and now I've found out about these letters Marcus's office received. What else is there I don't know?"

I open my eyes to see Shane frowning. "We'll work it out together. I'm with you all the way," he says.

"Thank you." I draw in a deep breath. What I need to do is change the subject. "So, where do you come from? New Zealand from the sounds of it."

Shane chuckles. "Got it in one. Usually I get mistaken for an Australian."

My stomach clenches as memories wash over me from back when Josh and I were friends. I was eighteen, had been in the same acting class as him, and was utterly besotted. I hadn't met a lot of good men by that stage, but I'd managed to surround myself with three of the best—Josh, Reece, and Clarke.

Even back then, Josh's star shone brighter than anyone else's.

But all he had to offer me was friendship.

He met Delaney and fell head over heels in love. I'm not

sure of the whole story, but I have a vivid memory of Clarke teasing him about his Kiwi goddess.

"Jessie? Did I lose you?"

I blink and look into Shane's face. His dark eyes take me in. "Sorry, it's just … I've been to New Zealand."

He leans back. "Really?"

"Filmed a movie there a few years ago. I didn't get a lot of sightseeing in. Flew in, shot the movie, and then left again. We stayed in a little town called Glenderry."

He nods slowly. "I know the area. The farm I live on isn't too far from there. Well, within a couple of hundred kilometres."

"Farm?" I catch my breath as a smile lights up his whole face. This farm must be something really special to him.

"Bunch of ex-army buddies and I bought it a few years ago. A couple of hundred cows, few sheep, handful of pigs and chickens. We started out with plans on growing the herd, but one of the guys is really into food science, so we started a bit of a side business making artisan products and that took over."

"Artisan products?"

He grins. "Cheese and bacon mostly. But one of the guys has really green fingers and we've put in a hothouse for him to see what he can grow to try new things to expand the range. One of my guys is a big fan of yours. I didn't tell him you were my assignment. He'd have kittens."

My cheeks burn hot. I'm well aware I have fans. They probably don't know what I'm like behind the scenes or don't care, but I know about the Facebook groups and the Twitter accounts that tweet good stuff. The good ones outnumber the bad, but it tends to be the bad that sticks in my mind.

"Well, I hope when this is all over and you tell him about me that he's still a fan."

Shane winks. "He's going to shit a brick if he catches any photos of us together."

"You should take a selfie with me and send it to him."

He shakes his head. "I'm no selfie taker."

"Give me your phone."

He unlocks it and hands it to me.

I hold it up, flipping the camera and leaning against him. "Say cheese."

I snap the photo and laugh when it comes up on the screen. I'm smiling widely, but Shane looks like he just swallowed razor blades.

"Do you want to try it again?" I ask.

"Shit, no," he mumbles.

I chuckle as I hand him the phone back. "There."

"Thank you. He's going to love it."

"You're welcome."

Heat radiates off him, and I'm drawn to it like a moth to a flame. I've never dealt with real relationships—sex has never had that emotional component to it for me, but Shane's the type of guy you snuggle with.

I don't do snuggling, but if he were here for any other reason than this, I might propose it.

Maybe I could be a *Netflix and chill* kind of girl after all.

"Did you pick a movie?" His question knocks me out of my thoughts.

"Yeah. I thought we could start the *Lord of the Rings* trilogy. See how far we get. I love those films."

He cocks an eyebrow. "Aren't they ridiculously long movies?"

"Yes and I love them. They're stunning. Maybe they'll make you feel at home."

Leaning his head on the back of the couch, he nods. "Whatever you want."

By the time the first movie's over, I'm stretched out on the couch and Shane's moved to a recliner to do the same. We're both full of pizza and my eyes keep trying to close.

"I think I'm going to get some sleep." I stand and stretch with a yawn.

"I'll just crash on the couch."

I look him up and down. "I don't know if you'll fit on my couch."

He shrugs. "On the floor, then."

"I do have a guest room."

Shane strokes his beard as if he's considering it. "I'm staying out here so I'll be between you and the front door."

"Whatever. I'll grab you a pillow and blankets." I head into the guest room, grab a blanket from the end of the bed and a couple of pillows, and bring them back out to the living room.

"Thank you." He takes them and our gazes lock. I'm so unsure how to read this man. He clearly takes his job seriously, and his first and only concern is my safety.

But the situation I'm in scares me and I learned a long time ago to swallow back my fear.

I need to let go and trust him even though I don't know him. And to me, that's just as scary as the threats against me.

"You okay?" His tone is so gentle. It's almost enough to make me cry.

Almost.

I shrug. "Yeah. I might not show it, but I'm glad you're here."

"I'm on your side, Jessie. Just remember that."

Bowing my head, I kick my toe into the carpet. "I know. I'll try and behave."

"I hope not."

My eyebrows twitch as I look back up. "What?"

"Your safety is my only concern. I'm looking forward to seeing you in action."

I clamp my lips together for a moment. "I assume you're talking about my reputation to be ..." I hold up my hands to air quote. "Be 'difficult.'"

He shakes his head. "I have no idea about your reputation, but you're a challenge, I can see that. I doubt I'm the only person you give shit to."

I chuckle. "Far from it."

"Goodnight, Jessie. Sleep well."

I pause for a moment. He turns to set up the couch, and I shift my gaze to the ceiling. I'm not sure what the next few days will bring with this guy following me around, but I do feel safer even with him on my couch.

Even if I'd prefer him in my bed.

Wait.

What?

This isn't that kind of situation. He's here to do a job. Nothing else. No matter how nice he is despite my bad attitude, I can't think that way about him.

8

———————

SHANE

Despite Jessie's few days off work being spontaneous, she's got an exercise class this morning.

I'd love an opportunity to get in a workout—especially after that pizza last night—but because I'm on babysitting duty, my job is to sit on my arse and keep an eye on her.

Walking into the gym is eye-opening.

The first thing I notice is the extreme blonde-to-brunette ratio. My previous visits to LA have been restricted to the client's house and occasionally an event. This is the first time I've really been out in the community.

I might be looking around to make sure Jessie's safe, but I don't miss the number of flirty smiles and glances headed my way. It's hard to avoid.

But there's only one woman I'm paying attention to, and it's the tall redhead walking in front of me.

She dressed before we left, pulling on sweatpants and a

sweatshirt. I'd asked her to prepare ahead of time rather than disappearing into a dressing room where I can't follow.

I'm not ready for the room we enter.

Three lines of five stripper poles fill the room.

"What kind of exercise class is this?" I ask.

Jessie shoots me a smug smile. "Pole dancing."

I nearly swallow my tongue.

A tall brunette in a leotard walks toward us.

"I'm sorry. No boyfriends allowed in this class. You'll have to wait outside. This class is women only."

I clamp my lips together in amusement.

"He's not my boyfriend; he's my bodyguard." Jessie crosses her arms.

The brunette raises an eyebrow and nods toward a chair against the wall by the door. "Then he sits over there."

"Fine with me," I say. "But I need to be able to see Jessie the whole time."

"That works. I'll just be at the back of the class." Jessie cocks her head.

Running both hands through my hair, I walk over to the chair the instructor pointed out. Jessie follows.

"At least I've got you to look after my things. The last gym I went to had a theft problem in the change rooms, and I had my bag stolen twice before they sorted it out."

I turn back toward her. "Why don't you have full-time security?"

She shrugs. "I'm a cheapskate."

Frowning, I take a seat. "But why?"

Jessie drops her bag beside me, and then reaches for the hem of her sweatshirt. In one swift move, she pulls it over her head and stands before me in a crop top. The sweat pants go next, and my eyes are stuck to her waist. There's nothing to her, but she's wearing hot pants, and I raise my gaze to meet hers.

A smirk graces her face. "Gotta get comfortable."

She drops the clothing she's removed on top of her bag. Turning around, she raises her arms above her head and stretches before leaning over to touch her toes.

Lord have mercy.

I don't know what I did to deserve this view, but I try to resist. It's impossible as she twists, stretching out her calves before standing straight.

My mouth's so dry, it's like the Sahara.

Jessie flicks me a smile over her shoulder before walking forward and grasping a pole.

Slowly, the class fills with beautiful women. I get some curious looks but continue to focus my gaze on Jessie who's doing some warm-up exercises.

I don't know if I can survive an hour of this class. There's a possibility my heart might beat so fast that it explodes.

The door's closed, and I pull out my phone. The room's lit softly, and the closed door shuts out the stark light from outside.

I shouldn't do it, but I can't help myself. I load up the farm WhatsApp group.

Me: You guys are never, ever going to guess where I am.

I blow out a breath as Jessie climbs and twirls down the pole.

Me: I'm sitting in a pole-dancing class watching Jessie Lane and about fifteen other gorgeous women shake their thangs

Digby: You bastard.

Cookie: Fuck me. Pics?

Me: a) That's a breach of privacy and b) I'd probably get thrown out. The instructor didn't want me here in the first place

Digby: You bastard.

Me: Hahaha I think I've broken Digby.

Digby: You bastard.

Ajax: Yep. It's official. Dig is broken.

I roll my eyes and look up in time to see Jessie upside down, one leg hooked around the pole, the other? Well, she's super flexible, and I'm not sure the human body is supposed to bend that way as she holds her foot in her hand, her leg arched backward behind her head.

Holy fuck.

Forget Digby. I think *I'm* broken looking at this.

Jessie's eyes meet mine, and she smiles at what I'm assuming is my stunned look before she whips her leg back to where it should be, and in an instant is the right way up and off the pole.

I'm not sure what the other women in the class are doing. I've got my eyes focused on what the hot redhead ... I mean, *client* right in front of me is doing.

She's so graceful.

It leaves me wondering what other skills she's learned over the years.

I shift in my seat as she performs a move that leaves me in no doubt as to how flexible she is.

This class has been running for five long minutes. There's another fifty-five minutes to go and I don't know if my cock can handle it.

I shouldn't feel this way. Not about a client.

But I have no choice but to watch and notice how supple Jessie is.

God damn it.

I'd cover my eyes, but there's no way out of this. How am I supposed to focus when ... holy shit.

She's upside down again.

I give in and just try to scan the room. But everywhere I look there are scantily clad, beautiful women doing things with their bodies that are a blessing to every hot-blooded straight man.

Although, this man could do with a break right now.

When the longest hour of my life is over, Jessie drops off the pole and saunters toward me.

"Have fun?" she asks.

"What was that move where your leg was hanging backward and looked like it should be broken?"

She doubles over laughing. "It's called the closed inside-leg hang. Why?"

I shrug. "Just looked complex. You must have a hell of a core."

Jessie grabs her towel from her bag and wipes her forehead with it. "If I'm doing something for a role, I like to nail it."

"For a role?"

She bites her bottom lip. "I'm playing a pole dancer in this movie I'm doing."

I swear to God, I nearly swallow my tongue. "Oh, so you're going back to work to do some more of this?"

She nods. "Nothing as high level as what I do here."

"Shame."

She laughs, placing her hand on my arm. "I'm sorry for dragging you here. It was clearly torture."

I shake my head as if trying to clear it. "I'm sure not going to forget it."

Jessie slams her other hand to her face and keeps on laughing while the other women leave the class, all watching us as they walk out the door.

"I should go to the changing room and get showered, but you can't follow me in there, so you'll have to deal with my sweaty body next to you in the car." Her eyes flash with amusement. She drops her hand.

I bend to pick up her bag. "I live with three other men on a farm. Sweat doesn't bother me."

"Oh, that's right." She turns to walk toward the door. "Your imaginary friends."

"I broke one of them telling him I was here with you."

She shoots an amused glance over her shoulder at me. "You broke him?"

"He thinks I'm a bastard." I follow her, and we walk out to her car with her laughing the whole way.

I've worked jobs where I've been bored to tears with how dry the people around me have been, but I've never worked one that's been this much fun.

Jessie might resent me tagging along everywhere with her, but she's no longer showing it—in fact, I think she set this gym visit up deliberately today given she was originally supposed to be on set. I chuckle to myself over her torturing me.

But it's made for an entertaining time, and keeping her

distracted from the seriousness of the situation is going to help.

There's nothing worse than a nervous client.

I'm not sure Jessie's ever been nervous. In the short time I've known her, I've observed that she just pushes forward.

I guess that's the confidence she's gotten from building the career she has. I've seen some of her movies, and I know she's worked with some of the biggest stars in Hollywood. She's got the celebrity attitude, but I stumble at the small apartment and cheaper car she drives.

Unlocking the car, I get into the driver's side as Jessie grumbles again. But she's got to get used to it. In fact, I'm still surprised she doesn't have her own security or driver already.

At least this time, when I start the car she doesn't make fun of me. Instead, she's quiet.

I'm not sure which Jessie I prefer.

9

———

SHANE

We stick close to the apartment the next couple of days before Jessie heads back to set.

And that's a bigger challenge.

It grinds my gears when I have to wait outside wardrobe. I'm employed to have eyes on Jessie, and that's not possible when she's getting changed. It's understandable, but also frustrating.

She emerges in a bathrobe.

"What's next?" I ask

"Makeup. And then I've got a scene to shoot, but it's not a long one. And then there's another one this afternoon."

I nod. "Tonight we'll go over your upcoming schedule if that's okay."

"Sure. There's a lot of waiting around. I hope you're prepared for that."

"It's not like I have anywhere else to be."

She snorts. "And I'm *such* great company."

"You're good at keeping me on my toes."

Taking a right turn, she heads into a Portacom marked makeup, with me on her heels.

A heavily made-up blonde who's doused in perfume presses a hand to my chest out of nowhere and brings me to a stop. "I'm sorry. You can't be in here."

"Just watch me."

Jessie snickers as she sits in a chair. "He's my bodyguard. Can't let me out of his sight or something."

"Can't you wait outside?" she asks.

I cross my arms. "No."

She narrows her eyes. "Fine. Just stand in the corner."

I smirk to piss her off, and it works because she storms off to the other side of the room.

Before too long, all the chairs are full and Jessie's tapping her fingernails impatiently on the bench in front of her.

My eyes are fixed on her. In a busy room, it's easy to lose track of what happens. I'm not too happy that she can't have her makeup done by herself, but I have to work with whatever I'm given.

I cringe when a woman walks up behind Jessie and places a hand on her shoulder.

"Don't touch me," Jessie shrieks.

The makeup lady takes a step back and holds her hands up. "I'm sorry ... I—"

"I don't care. I want someone else to do my makeup." Jessie crosses her arms and turns to face the mirror.

"I'm sorry, Ms Lane. I didn't mean to upset you. Everyone else is busy, and I've done your makeup before. Could we please ...?"

Jessie waves her away with a flick of the wrist. "Find someone else to do it. Now."

Whoa. There it is. Marcus told me she could act like a diva. Maybe this whole thing has her more worried than I realised.

"Jessie," I call across the room. "You okay?"

She looks across at me, her face tight with tension. "Fine."

My eyebrows rise. "You sure? Has something happened?"

Jessie shakes her head. "No. I just don't like being touched without warning."

I frown. There's an edge to her tone I don't like. Walking over to her, I crouch in front of the chair. "I'm going to ask you again. Are you okay?"

She clenches her jaw. "Last time I was here was the whole rat in the trailer thing. I'm on edge."

I nod. "I bet. But I'm here, and I'm not about to let anything happen to you. How about you let the lady do her job?"

She squeezes her hands into fists before letting out a long breath and looking over her shoulder at the makeup lady. "I'm sorry. Can we start again?"

The woman flicks a gaze between us and nods slowly. I'm not sure how much other people on set know about what happened the other day, but I step back and let her get to work.

"I'm not far if you need me. You're safe."

I give her what I hope is a reassuring smile, and make a mental note to talk to Jessie later about this. We've bantered a bit, but her reaction to what happened seems out of proportion. Has something else happened she hasn't told Marcus or me about?

There's only one entrance, and I keep an eye on it in when I'm not watching the makeup artists work.

And they are artists.

Jessie's transformed into her character, the contours of her face highlighted, the smokiness of her eyes alluring, and I can't take my eyes off her red lips.

She's naturally a beautiful woman, but she really does look like someone else just by having her makeup done.

Jessie rises from her chair, and walks toward me.

"You ready?" she asks.

"Always. You?"

"I've gotta get to set. I'll show you where to sit and you can look after my robe."

I cross my arms and nod slowly. "So, now I'm your wardrobe assistant?"

"You're anything I want you to be as long as I'm paying the bills."

Meow.

I frown. "Are you okay?"

She nods, averting her gaze to anywhere but me.

"Are you sure? Something happened earlier. Does that still have you on edge?"

Jessie purses her red-painted lips. "I'm fine."

She's anything but fine, but I'll let it slide. For now. "Come on, your majesty," I say.

Her lips curl into a smile. "This way, caveman."

We step back out into the sunshine and walk toward a large shed. It looks cold and unwelcoming from the outside, but once Jessie opens the door and walks inside, I catch my breath.

Cameras and equipment are everywhere, but the set is all muted pink and purple tones and is the replica of any strip bar I've been to. Two stages with poles are at one end, and circular tables fill the room.

For all my previous work, I've never been on a movie set. I guess this is where the magic happens.

"Hold my robe? My chair's over there if you want to sit down." Jessie shoves the garment into my hand and points toward a wall. "It's got my name on the back of it if you're confused."

I cock my head. "I'm sure I can find it."

She steps out from beside me.

Holy shit.

Jessie Lane is a goddess.

She stands before me in some tiny sparkling silver hot pants, her long, tanned legs seeming to go on forever. On top, she's wearing a light pink crop top that moulds to her breasts.

If I wasn't professional, I'd be wiping the drool from my lips. But I am, so I take in the sight of her and force a slight smile.

"I'm a pole dancer," she says. "This is like a modernised version of *Pretty Woman.*"

"I think *Pretty Woman* still holds up pretty well."

She smirks. "I'm not debating this with you right now. I have a scene to shoot."

"You dancing today?" I ask, trying to keep the hope out of my voice.

Jessie laughs. "No. This is an emotional scene, believe it

or not. Maybe we should have waited until today to take that selfie for your ..." She waggles her fingers making air quotes. "... 'friend.'"

"You really think I have no friends?"

She shrugs. "The more I think about it, the more I wonder."

"Digby will be devastated." I hold my hand to my heart.

Jessie pats me on the shoulder. "Have I told you how sweet it is that your imaginary friend has a name?"

I can't help but laugh. Even when she's trying to be bitchy, it's amusing. The scene she made in the makeup trailer was a different situation though, and it makes me wonder what she's hiding beneath the attitude.

Finding her chair, I take a seat and watch as they set up the scene.

Of the actors around, I do recognise Declan O'Leary. He made a series of war films a few years ago that the boys really enjoyed.

He flashes Jessie a smile that I'm sure charms the panties off women. My blood boils. It shouldn't. I'm nothing to Jessie. Her life is right here on this set

Shit.

Am I going to have to watch them kissing?

I'm not sure I can deal with that.

I'm not even sure where these thoughts come from when she is the client, I am the employee, and she's driven me nuts so far.

Deliberately.

Silence descends the set.

It's like Jessie transforms the second the scene starts.

She's mesmerising as she becomes someone else right in front of my eyes. It's an emotional scene. I don't know anything about the movie, but I can't take my eyes off Jessie the whole time.

I can almost forget my growing attraction to her when she and Declan embrace.

Almost.

When the director calls, "cut," her expression blanks for a moment and a scowl takes over. I can't help but smile. *That's my girl.*

She fixes her gaze on the director as he walks over to congratulate her on nailing her scene. Marcus had told me her last day on set was disrupted when she was upset by the rat, and I frown at the impact it must have had on her.

Once she's done, she's standing in front of me, reaching for her robe.

"One more scene for the day and that's me." She tightens the robe around her.

"That's it?"

"If we can nail it quickly like we did that one, then we'll be home early. Declan's a pro. At least he's easy to work with." She sighs. "I can't wait for this day to be over. The sooner I can get into some real clothes, the better."

I chuckle. "It's not much different to what you wore at the gym."

She looks up at me. "Yeah, but being on camera with my ass hanging out is different to the privacy of the gym."

My chest tightens at the memory of Cookie asking for pictures in the class. I never would have breached anyone's privacy, but even being asked for it feels tacky.

"You know, one of my friends asked for pictures of you in that class."

She comes to a stop and narrows her eyes. "You didn't …"

"No. I didn't. And I wouldn't. He knows I wouldn't. But I feel bad for even the suggestion."

Jessie shrugs. "You didn't do anything. It's okay."

"Yeah, but I still feel bad."

"Why?" Those green eyes search mine.

"I don't know? But what I do know is that I'd never do anything like that without your permission. I hope you know that."

A smile tugs at her lips. "I've got no reason not to trust you."

We walk a little farther together before turning a corner.

Jessie gasps, and I follow her gaze to where she's looking.

The lock hangs useless on her trailer door.

I grasp her arm. "I'll go in first."

She nods and stands back as I walk up the steps.

I step into the trailer and look for anything different or out of place. This shouldn't be the case because we were only in here a short time ago, and no one should have access to her space.

I scan the interior of the trailer. Nothing seems to be out of place until I reach the table.

My eyes narrow as I take in a photo of Jessie. It's not from today because the costume is different, but it was definitely taken on the set we were just on.

A knife sits buried in the table straight through Jessie's head.

I look around for a note, but there doesn't appear to be one.

I'm not sure that there needs to be as the threat is clear.

I pull my phone out and dial Marcus. Leaving a message for him, I step back outside.

Security arrives, and Jessie wraps her arms around herself as she watches the trailer intently.

I leave them to check it out while walking over to her.

"What is it?" she asks.

"A threat. No animals this time. But nothing I want you to see."

Her throat tightens. "Is it bad?"

"It's no worse than the others?" I take a risk and brush my hands down her arms. She shivers, but she doesn't lose her shit. "You're safe, Jessie. We just need to find somewhere else for you to wait until you're needed on set. Okay?"

If it were anyone else, I'd think she needed a hug, but I'm not sure when it comes to Jessie, and I still have to honour the line between us.

Declan walks around the corner and pauses. "What's going on here?"

"Some psycho keeps sending me love notes," Jessie mumbles.

"Want to use my trailer in the meantime? We're not due back on set for another hour."

He winks at her, and I grit my teeth.

He's just her co-star. Not that you should be thinking that way about her.

The head of security walks toward us. I don't pause to greet him, clenching my fist in anger as he approaches.

"Where's the security on the trailers?" I ask.

He sniffs. "We have fences, and there are guards on the entrance. No one gets on set without prior permission."

"So it's someone on set who's threatening Jessie?"

He shuffles his feet. "I guess ... it must ..."

"Some head of security you are."

Jessie snorts, and he shoots a glare at her.

"I want eyes on that trailer twenty-four hours a day. Don't care how you do it. I want to know if anyone comes within fifty feet of it. That's the least you can do around here."

"You paying for that?"

"If I have to." I stare him down until he shrugs. Apart from paying me, Marcus set a budget for any extra services I might need, but she should feel safe in her workplace so they should make sure she's covered.

"We've got security cameras set up on the gate. Adding a couple more won't be too hard."

I nod. "Good. Do it."

Jessie places a hand on my bicep as he walks away. "Can't you tell me what it was? I really want to know."

"Nothing you need to see."

She sniffs and I turn my head to look at her, but her expression gives away nothing.

"Do you trust me?" I ask.

She meets my gaze. "With my life."

"Then let's get you to Declan's trailer while the police come and sort all this out. Hopefully by the time you've finished working, you'll have your trailer back."

"Come on, babe. Let's get a drink before we have to head

back to set." Declan's lazy smile rankles me, but I've got no reason to lash out at him.

Jessie lights up. "I'm not one for day drinking, but I think this is a special occasion."

I grimace and follow Declan and Jessie to his trailer.

Declan opens the door.

"Do you need anything out of your trailer?"

Jessie shakes her head. "Not right now."

"Go inside and I'll be back as soon as I've finished speaking with the police." I fix my gaze on Declan. "I'm trusting you to stay with her until I'm back."

He nods. "You have my word."

I turn to Jessie. "And you, stay put."

She waves me away. "Of course, you sweet-talking devil."

Declan chuckles and ushers Jessie inside, winking at me as he does. I shoot him a death glare and turn back to go and talk to the police.

I don't want to leave her, but this has to stop—and that starts with me making sure those new cameras go up *today*.

By the time I'm finished, Declan and Jessie are ready to head back to set.

I trail along behind them, my teeth grinding as Declan flirts up a storm with Jessie. There's no sign that they've been drinking, but Jessie's giggling, and I'd rather think that it's because she's had a drink than because his flirting is working.

Taking a seat, I catch her robe when she throws it at me.

"Look after that, would you?" she asks.

A quick touch-up of her makeup and she transforms into this vulnerable woman who's found love but is painfully aware of the differences between her and the businessman she's fallen for.

Once again, she's flawless in her scene.

But the moment she's finished, her shoulders slump and she lets out a sigh of relief.

"Great work, Jessie," the director says. "I know that things are tough for you right now, but you're on fire."

Her whole face lights up in a smile. "Thank you."

"Have a good sleep, and we'll see you all again tomorrow."

Declan grabs her hand, and Jessie snaps back, her eyes wide. He holds up his palms. "Sorry. I know you don't like being touched."

"Sorry. It's just ..." She swallows hard. "I'm a little wound up after the scene. I'm fine."

He frowns. "Are you sure? I'm sorry. I thought you might want to go for a drink."

"Thanks, but I'm ready to go home. It's fine."

The way she stalks toward me, her arms wrapped around herself, tells me she's not fine at all.

"Get me out of here," she murmurs as I slide her robe around her shoulders.

"Whatever you need."

It's not until we're back inside her apartment that she finally breaks down.

It's been bubbling away since we left the set, but as soon as we step in the door, she bursts into tears.

And despite picking up that she doesn't like being touched, I pull her into my arms and let her rest her head on my chest.

For the first time, she doesn't flinch or shudder; she slouches, and hot tears wet my shirt as she lets it all out.

I walk her over to the couch and pull her onto my lap. I don't care if it's unprofessional. I don't care if I'm overstepping a mark.

Jessie needs someone to be on her side. Not just because of these threats, but because she needs a friend. It's clear to me that other than Marcus, she has no one.

That shouldn't be my problem, but I'm making it mine.

"Why is this happening?" she whispers.

I cup her face. "We'll work it out. And we'll stop it. I want you to know that I'm here, Jessie, and I'm not going anywhere until it's over. You've got me."

She sniffs and rests her head on my shoulder. "You're not so bad for a Neanderthal."

"You're not so bad for a spoiled Hollywood princess."

"Don't make me laugh, I'll end up with a snot bubble."

I bark out a laugh. "You do that and I might have to learn how to take photos with this damn phone. We'd break the internet."

Jessie shakes against me with laughter. "I'm not so sure about that."

"Got you laughing. That's all that matters."

She pulls her head back and looks at me with a pinched expression. "I'm still not sure what to make of you."

"That makes two of us, sweetheart."

10

When Marcus inserted Shane into my life, I was mad about it. I knew it was for my own safety, but I resented the disruption even more than the threats that scared me.

But after our moment on the couch, I don't hate having him around so much. And he is good at blending into the background, for a guy of his size. I can't really argue that his presence is interfering with my social life because I'd have to have one in the first place for that to be true.

After three weeks of having him on my tail, I've grown accustomed to having his presence. I don't know if I'd call us friends, but we've formed a mutual respect for one another. It turns out he can be a calming influence—right when I need it.

Finishing this movie can't come soon enough. Then I can retreat to the safety of my home.

I've had a heavy day and we're heading back to my trailer again before going home for the weekend.

I'm dead on my feet.

For a movie that's going nowhere, it's been a lot of hard work. Thankfully the shoot won't be long, because I'm over the whole thing and ready to take a break.

The only good thing is that it's been three weeks since we last heard from my little friend. No letters, no notes, and I'm not sure whether to be relieved or concerned by the silence.

"Pizza for dinner tonight?" I ask Shane.

"Sounds good to me. I'm starved. What toppings are you thinking?"

I roll my eyes as a woman waves at him from the catering tent.

She's taken a liking to him and keeps showing up to bring him food. He keeps turning down her offers of a date because he says he needs to treat everyone with suspicion.

I'm sure he just doesn't want to flirt in front of me.

Whether that's for professional or personal reasons, I'm not sure.

But increasingly, I hope it's the latter.

He nudges my arm. "You okay?"

I blink a bunch of times. Clearly I've been lost in my own head again. "Sorry. What?"

"What kind of pizzas are you thinking? I wouldn't mind trying something different. Bit over the old pepperoni."

I shrug. "Whatever you feel like. I've got a menu some-where, but it's probably online."

He walks a little ahead of me and opens my trailer door. "Motherfu—"

"What is it?"

Shane looks back over his shoulder. "Your trailer's been trashed. There's no threat that I can see, but it's a mess in there. Let's call security and get them to take over and then just get out of here."

I cross my arms, gripping them tight across my chest.

"Take a step back," Shane murmurs.

"But—"

"You don't need to see this."

He turns toward me and grasps my biceps. I stopped flinching whenever he touches me a while ago. I'm well aware that's significant for me.

"Too late. I've already seen it." I meet his gaze. "How did they get in here. Again?"

He shakes his head. "I don't know. I'll get the security company to go over the CCTV."

He pulls me around and steadies me. I blow out a shaky breath.

Shane makes me feel safe. It's something I haven't felt in years, but I never realised that until now. I've been cautious with who I've been involved with because there have been very few men in my life who have made me feel this way.

Shane's not my friend. He's employed to keep me safe, and I can see by the way his jaw tics that he's not impressed at the lack of support he seems to be getting.

"I need to make a phone call and we'll get you home." His tone is so gentle. It takes a lot to shake me, and while the previous threats left me rattled, this one feels way more personal.

I nod.

He pulls out his phone.

"Jessie." I turn to see Clay, the director, walking toward me and frowning. "What's happened?"

"This." I wave behind me.

As he reaches me, he looks into the trailer and gapes. "Oh my God. I knew you had extra security for a reason, but this is the first time I've seen anything." He meets my gaze. "Are you okay?"

"Not really?"

He scowls. "We'll lock down the set. Essential staff only."

"Won't that cause delays?"

He nods. "It's not a long shoot. If it takes a little more time to get things done, then that's what it takes. The studio will complain, but we're so close to being done, and we've only got one leading lady."

Tears take me by surprise, and I try to blink them away.

"Jessie," he says gently. "You were my only choice for this film. Your audition is one of the best I've ever seen. Don't let this shit get you down."

I sniff. "Thank you."

He walks away, barking orders at people, and I know he'll do whatever he can to keep me safe. And he's wrong. The reason I wanted this job originally is because I saw the potential in this film and the possibility for it to move my career in the right direction.

People like nostalgia, even if it feels like a rip-off of an earlier hit. Of course, that was before it turned out to likely be a straight-to-video release.

Shane glances over his shoulder toward me, his mobile

phone pressed to his ear. "As soon as this movie is finished filming, I'm getting her out of here."

I bite my bottom lip. He must be more worried than he's letting on.

"Whoever this is, they seem to have ready access to this set and fuck knows where else, so we're getting out of town. I'll take her home if I need to."

Home?

He chuckles. "She's freaked out, Marcus, and I don't blame her. We'll go somewhere safe while you get this shit investigated and solved. Hire PIs, do whatever it takes, but you put me in charge of her safety, and that's my recommendation."

My heart thuds. I know it's his job, but there's a part of me that wants to believe this is personal—that Shane wants to protect me because it's more than just work. He's seen me at my worst though, and I know that isn't pretty.

He ends the call and turns toward me. "Do you have a valid passport?"

I stare at him. "Of course. I made a movie in France last year, and—"

"Good. Once this movie is done, let's grab it. You pack a bag, and we'll get out of here."

My eyes widen. "Where are we going?"

"My farm."

I let out a nervous laugh. "We're going to the other side of the world?"

"I know it's extreme, but the way things have been here, I know you'll be safe." His dark eyes bore a hole in my brain.

"Besides, I know you have an empty schedule, and I have cows to milk."

"Oh, so we're going there because it's convenient for you." I drop my hands to my hips.

"My business partners can manage things for themselves, but they won't say no to extra help." He raises his hand to cup my jaw, his thumb resting on my cheek. "Marcus agrees. We need you safe."

We.

"Maybe I just don't want to go. Can't we go somewhere else?" My last visit to New Zealand didn't end the way I'd hoped. I'd thought filming a romantic movie with Josh might make him finally see me. Instead, he ended up finding Delaney and, well, the rest is history.

Shane huffs out a breath. "If this person can get to your trailer despite all the security, they can get to you. I'm concerned, as is Marcus, that this is someone in the industry. Someone you clearly don't suspect. So I'm all for taking you as far away as we can get while he focuses efforts on the investigation."

"I'll be safe?"

He runs his thumb down my cheek. It's an intimate gesture, but not one that makes me uncomfortable. This man has been living in my apartment this past month, and we've tolerated each other. I know I can trust him.

"You'll be safe."

"With your imaginary friends?"

He drops his hand and smirks at me. "Yeah, something like that."

For a moment, we just gaze at one another. What do I

really have to lose? I can make audition tapes from anywhere. And it's not like I have any projects lined up. A break might just do me some good.

My trailer's crawling with security, but I can't focus on anything but the blood rushing in my ears.

"You know, Jessie, I'm an arsehole," Shane lowers his voice.

I frown. "What? Why? I think it's a little insane for us to travel that far, but it also makes sense to me."

"No. Not that." His heated gaze runs over my face, and my cheeks heat. "I just touched you. I keep doing it, and I know you don't like that without warning."

I blink rapidly. "I ... it's fine."

But my stomach flips at the thought. There are very few people in my life who I don't mind touching me without asking, and they're people I've known for years.

Reece is one of them.

Josh would be, too, if he came anywhere near me.

Clarke used to be, but I haven't seen him in what feels like years.

Marcus is like family.

And now I can apparently add Shane to that list.

I'm not too sure how I feel about that.

11

JESSIE

By the time we reach the end of the shoot, I'm on my last nerve.

We're no closer to finding out who this person harassing me is. The day of the last incident with my trailer, the newly installed security cameras were down for maintenance.

The circle's so tight; no one should have known that. I thought that this would be the time they'd be caught, but as it turns out, everyone's as clueless about who's after me as they were when this started.

I'm tired from lack of sleep.

And my hot pants are crawling up my ass today.

When Clay calls "cut" on the last scene, I all but run for my robe and hightail it to my trailer.

Shane calls my name as I shoot past him to my trailer, getting inside and closing the door behind me.

He bangs on the door, but I just need a moment to change into my clothing and feel like me again.

"Jessie. Open up."

"I'll be out in a minute."

I have privacy in my trailer, even with him in it as it has a decent sized bedroom for me to change in, but I haven't had a real moment to myself in weeks.

Stripping off my costume for the last time, I throw it on the floor and tug on a pair of jeans. Slipping on a bra and T-shirt, I let out a yawn. At least when we travel, I'll get time to rest and sleep.

Grabbing my bag, I unlock the door and open it.

Shane stands outside, his arms crossed and his jaw set.

"Did you want to go for a drink with the cast and crew?" he asks.

I roll my eyes. "One and then we're out of here."

The last thing I need is people grumbling that I didn't stick around or that I'm not a team player. In all of this, my career's still on the line.

When we reach the area where everyone's gathering, someone tries to hand me a beer, and Shane puts a stop to it.

"We'll get a sealed one. Just to be safe," he says.

I scrub my face with my hands before nodding.

A hand lands on my shoulder, and I grit my teeth.

"It was good working with you."

I blow out a relieved breath at Declan O'Leary's dulcet tones. "You too."

He drops his hand. "I know you're under some pressure. Hope things get sorted out."

"This whole stalker thing is dragging on, so I'm leaving

town for a while." I take a deep breath. "What are your plans?"

He shrugs. "Might go to Vegas, get blitzed for the weekend. Then come home and work out what I'm doing for the rest of my life because I'm not sure if it's this."

Frowning, I grip his forearm. "I'm so sorry. You're such a huge talent. You were one of my favourite actors when I was growing up."

Declan smirks. "Way to make me feel old."

I smile sweetly. "You shouldn't feel that way. I've loved making this movie with you."

Damn it.

I wish I was on good terms with Josh. Maybe I could have pointed Declan in his direction. Declan's just fallen on hard times—he was one of the finest actors of his generation.

He clearly needs a boost, but I have no influence to help him or I'd be helping myself.

"Appreciate that." He takes a sip of beer. "What about you? How'd you end up on this shit show of a movie?"

I laugh. "I'm a fuck-up. Now I've got to try and be nice to people to dig myself out of the hole I'm in. Maybe taking some time out will help."

Declan leans in and pecks me on the cheek. "Maybe. I'm going to get out of here and start planning a weekend of debauchery. Take care, Jessie."

My heart flutters. He really is sweet and far too good for this movie. "You too."

He walks away, and I stand there for a moment just taking some deep breaths.

"Everything okay?" Shane asks, moving to my side. He cracks open a bottle of beer and hands it to me.

"Not really." I take a long drink.

"After this, we should get out of here and pack," he says softly.

I nod. "Sure thing."

"Pizza?" he asks as we approach my apartment door.

I look over my shoulder as I turn the key. "No, I'm cooking tonight. Won't be anything fancy, but I can make a real good ramen noodle."

"Wow. You really are a cheapskate."

Shane has been teasing me about my cheap ways since he got here. And in some things, he's probably justified. I am reckless with my security. I have people who take care of things like my social media presence, and fan-related things like signed photos.

I push open the door and freeze.

My couch cushions lay on the floor, ripped open, their fluffy white filling spread in clumps across the carpet. The coffee table lays on its side, and ...

Shane grabs my arms and spins me around. "We're going to stay in a hotel for the night. Okay?"

I nod. This is even more personal than the trailer—this is my home.

"Stay right here."

Numbness creeps up my body. The code was changed.

Whoever this is, they either had a key or picked the lock to get in.

I press my hand to my chest as my heart races.

Shane enters my apartment and I draw in deep breaths. There's no one in the corridor with me, but am I safe here? My breathing speeds up, and my head swims.

A hand lands on my shoulder.

I yelp, and Shane backs up, palms raised.

"I'm sorry. Is there anything in there you need?"

"Clothing."

He chews his lip. "About that."

"Fuck." I screech. "Everything?"

His brows knit. "Seems to be. Everything in your wardrobe is shredded. I'm not sure about the drawers."

I take in a deep breath. "The wardrobe's all my evening things anyway. I just need some more things like this." Waving a hand to indicate my sweats, I meet Shane's gaze.

"I'm calling Marcus to make sure we get the detective working the case down here. And then I'm going to secure you in a hotel while they do what they have to."

"But I want my stuff."

He nods. "I know you do, but they need to come in and dust for prints. The less we touch, the better. We'll come back when they're done."

"Do we really have to stay in a hotel?"

"Now's not the time for your cheapskate ways." His lopsided smile would normally make my heart beat faster, but this time, I see red.

"Is this really a good time to make fun of me?" I yell.

His expression falls. "I'm not making fun of you, Jessie.

I'm trying to shift your focus to other things so you don't freak out."

"It's too late for that." Shane wraps his large frame around mine, and I breathe in his earthy scent.

"I'm sorry," he murmurs. "You act so tough all the time, and I forget you're a big softy under that rock-hard exterior."

I pull back and glare at him. "Could you do that with a little less sarcasm?"

"I'm not being sarcastic. I see you, Jessie Lane." His dark eyes are enough to melt into.

Not that I can.

Not that I will.

"No one ever *sees* me."

"I do."

I gulp. He's driven me mad with the way he's always there, even though it's what he's with me for. I'm used to being under the spotlight—not so used to anyone really working me out. Not even my best friends have ever done that.

But Shane? Shane's different.

I back away and place a hand on his arm. "Thank you for caring."

"It's my job."

My heart sinks, but he's right. This is his job. He's not being my friend—he's being the bodyguard employed to keep me safe.

He wouldn't really want me in any other way.

Not if he knew who I really was.

12

SHANE

Two days later, we're on a flight to New Zealand.

It's a relief when we finally hand over our boarding passes and step onto the plane. I'm looking forward to going home and introducing Jessie to my boys. Digby will have kittens. The thought of that brings a grin to my face.

After a lot of fuss, Marcus had the tickets booked, and I'm bemused to find we're sitting near the front of the plane.

So much for not attracting attention.

I wait until the plane is in the air.

"Business class?" I ask.

Jessie shrugs. "They don't have first class on this flight, so I settled."

I roll my eyes. "This is supposed to be low-key."

"So are you, but look at you all hulking around like the Hulk."

Chuckling, I shake my head. "I can't make myself physically smaller."

Her eyes sparkle with amusement. "Maybe not, but it's not just your physical presence. You exude power."

It's hard not to roll my eyes again, but I resist the urge and raise my eyebrows instead.

"I'd be scared shitless of you if I thought you weren't on my side." She shoots me a wink and pulls an eye mask on before lying down. "Wake me up when we get there."

I chuckle and shake my head.

I've never been good at sleeping on planes. If I had to identify the one thing in my life that makes me nervous, it'd be flying. Not that I'd ever admit it.

At least on the flight it'll be easy to keep an eye on Jessie—especially if she sleeps the whole time.

Jessie nestles down into the plane bed, pulling a blanket over her.

"I'll wake you when we get there, Princess Jessie."

"Finally," she mumbles.

I don't have the heart to tell her that she snores.

Jessie wakes up with two hours to go on our flight.

I'm not sure I've ever met anyone who sleeps the way she does. It seems to be nothing for her to lie down and just sleep for hours whereas I'm lucky to get six hours at night, and I'm not one to nap.

She yawns. "Where are we?"

"About two hours from Auckland. How was your sleep?"

"Could have been about two hours longer." A smile graces her lips. "I could do with a drink."

"Push the button and everything you want will be provided." I chuckle.

She rolls her eyes and casts her gaze across the overflowing tray in front of me. "I can see you've been making the most of it."

"I've never flown business class internationally. I figure I might as well get your money's worth. Someone had to eat what was on offer, and you were asleep the whole time."

Jessie laughs. "Was the food good at least?"

"I'm sure there's still time for you to have some."

She shakes her head. "I'm dehydrated. I just need some water. Besides, I'm looking forward to landing and ordering room service when we get to the hotel."

I smirk. While I'd wanted to do the whole trip as quickly as possible, Jessie held out for a night in Auckland before we travelled on to the farm. We'll be sharing a room, so I don't have too much of an issue with the delay, and the thought of sitting back and ordering room service sounds good to me.

Besides, there are another two flights ahead of us, and a night's rest will be good before we hit home.

Jessie might live frugally, but she's used to the good things in life. I already know she'll be spoiled rotten on the farm, but she'll have to work too.

Once we've landed, we take a taxi to a nearby hotel. I'm not surprised to find out she's booked a room with twin queen beds. She's a walking contradiction, splurging on the airfares then getting a fairly standard room. But it's warm and comfortable, and we can settle in for the night.

"Which bed do you want?" she asks.

"It doesn't matter. Take your pick." I wave toward the mattresses.

"This one." She picks the right, and flops down, letting out a long breath. "I hate flying."

"It's not really my favourite thing either." I step further into the room and cross my arms.

Jessie sits up. "Why did you take the job?"

My eyebrows rise. "Babysitting you?"

Her lips purse. "If you want to see it that way."

I shrug. "Money's good. Marcus has never screwed me over. Why do you ask?"

She kicks off her shoes. "Just wondering. You seem to be going to a lot of effort."

"Why wouldn't I?" I step into the room. "My job is taking care of you and making sure you're safe."

Nodding, she sits up, pulling her knees into her chest, wrapping her arms around them and rocking. For a moment, she looks so childlike. Her brow furrows, and she curls up tight. "Do you still think you can do that?"

I cross the room and sit on the end of the bed. "I'll do my very best. I know you're unsure about going to the farm, but my whole intent is to get you somewhere I can lock down myself."

"I'm okay about coming here. To be honest, it's nice to have a change of scene." She releases her grip on her knees. "More than just these stupid threats."

Frowning, I scoot up the bed and wrap an arm around her. This is the second time I've done something like this. It's not professional, but right now, I don't care. This whole time,

I've sensed there was more to her fear than the security issues—she's running on empty.

For an instant, she freezes, but then she leans her head on my shoulder.

"Tell me?" I croak.

She wraps her arms around my chest and buries herself in deeper. "You don't want to know."

"I might surprise you."

"Can we just stay like this a while?" Her voice shakes, and I draw in a deep breath and pull her into my arms. When was the last time someone held her like this?

All this time spent together, and I'm still none the wiser about the mystery that is Jessie Lane. What I do know is that she's built barriers around herself. I'm not sure what she's protecting, or who, but she's a lot smarter and deeper than people give her credit for. But she hides behind this facade of being a brat.

She lets out a sigh, and I close my eyes. I've been with my share of women, and I'm not sure I've ever held one like this when we haven't shared intimacies. But Jessie's a client, and I'm crossing the line.

"Come here." I lie down, pulling her with me, and she rolls until her back's to me and I can spoon her. Placing a hand on her stomach, I pull her in tight against me. "Sleep."

Jessie yawns and murmurs something about me being a bossy asshole. I chuckle softly as her breathing slows and she's out like a light.

I know she's likely jetlagged, but has she been sleeping back in the States? This whole situation can't have been easy on her. Fresh air and farm living for a while will do her some good. The boys and I'll work to distract her from her troubles and keep her safe.

I'm not afraid to admit that this is more than a job now. I've never hugged a client let alone spooned them while they slept.

Jessie Lane makes me want to cross those invisible lines that have always kept my work and home life separate. Hell, taking her to the farm is a big breach of my personal rules.

But I'll do whatever it takes to keep her safe.

And not just because I'm being paid.

13

———————

JESSIE

I 'm wrapped in a cocoon of warmth and I don't want to move.

Our flight to the South Island of New Zealand is this afternoon, so there's no need for me to hurry out of bed.

Shane murmurs in his sleep, his chest rumbling against my back.

I didn't ask for any of this, but I'm glad Shane's been brought into my life. I'm not sure if I'd exactly call us friends, but finding someone I can trust isn't common, and while I don't want to let him know I cherish him being around, that's how I feel.

The fact I'm paying him to be with me is pushed to the back of my mind.

But this? This he isn't paid for. He saw me struggling last night and he comforted me. That's priceless. That's something I've rarely had in my life. I didn't even need to ask for help.

I see you, Jessie Lane.

His words have stuck with me ever since he said them, and I'm starting to believe them. What people usually see is my outside shell. I'm bossy, angry at times, and hate being touched, but delve deeper and I'm sensitive.

I hear the whispers about my behaviour.

I feel the barbs.

I know I'm not liked.

This whole situation has stripped me raw, and Shane sees that.

I roll over and watch him sleep. The stress lines that worry his forehead are relaxed for the first time since we've met. Maybe being so far from LA has eased the tension.

Gently, I brush my fingers down his cheek.

Our pizza nights and the way he comforts me have burrowed into my heart, and I don't want to let that feeling go.

Conflict rages in my head over trusting someone new.

But I'm also short on people who care about me, and I think—*hope* that this is more than a job for him now.

Old me would be making a move for sex.

This version of me isn't so sure. Especially when technically he's working for me.

His eyes flicker open and he gives me a lazy smile. "Good morning."

"Morning."

"Sleep well?"

"Better than I have in ages," I whisper.

"Me too." He lets out a sigh. "I shouldn't have done this, though."

I chew the inside of my cheek. "I know, but I'm grateful."

He's off the bed in an instant and looking down at me. "Room service? I could do a full English breakfast."

My stomach grumbles. "Oooh me too."

"I'll get the order placed."

I roll onto my back and close my eyes. I'm still tired, but a good breakfast should set me up for the day. We've got a lot of traveling to do, but at least the worst of it is over.

Maybe I should have negotiated a few days here so I could just stay in this bed.

I doze until Shane gently shakes me awake. "Breakfast is here."

I wolf down the scrambled eggs and bacon, then lean back and pat my stomach. "I needed that."

Shane's still eating, but puts his knife and fork down. "You must have been hungry."

"It's the jetlag. And all the sleep. It always makes me hungry."

He fights a grin. "I can tell you now there's plenty of food where we're going. Cookie will spoil you rotten."

"Cookie?"

Shane picks up his fork and stabs at a slice of bacon. "He did his chef's training in the army. Now he feeds us."

"So I have access to an on-call chef?"

He laughs. "Good luck waking him up once he's asleep, but sure."

I bite my bottom lip. "Thank you for this. I hope you know I'm feeling safer already."

Shane drops his fork on the plate with a clatter. He stands and walks around the table. "I'm glad."

I swallow hard. He's there. Right there. I want to wrap my arms around him and close my eyes. It's not where we are—it's who I'm with. He makes me feel safe.

He reaches down and runs his thumb over my cheek. "I shouldn't do this," he says.

"No, you shouldn't."

His thumb traces along my bottom lip. My heart pounds at his touch, and then his hand's gone just as fast as it arrived.

"When this is all over, I hope we're still friends," I whisper.

He chuckles. "The princess and the Neanderthal."

My lips twitch. "Something like that."

"We should get moving. Our flight to Christchurch is in an hour and a half, and we're supposed to check in at least thirty minutes prior."

I cock an eyebrow. "The airport's right over there," I point in the direction I hope it's in.

He chuckles. "Yes, but you still need to get ready and if I've learned anything about you, it's that it could take that whole hour and a half."

Narrowing my gaze, I rise from the table. "Will not."

"Your shower will take half an hour alone."

I slap his butt as I walk away and he chuckles.

"All the goodwill you generated last night is gone," I call.

I close the bathroom door to the sound of his laughter.

14

SHANE

Jessie looks around the room, and I cringe inside.

Four men live in this house, and none of us care about having the newest of things. It's clean and tidy, but the furnishings are old and weren't new when we bought them. The big leather couch in the living room has tears in it and stuffing hangs out on one end. The rugs covering the wooden floors are threadbare in parts. But it's homely and comfortable and everything we need at the end of a long day on the farm.

And she'll just have to deal with it until we catch this person harassing her.

Jessie blanks her expression, but not before I see the look of distaste on her face.

"Is everything okay, your highness?" I ask.

Her glare sets me on fire. "I'm just wondering why ..." She looks back at the kitchen. "... that room is shiny and looks new, and this one looks like it spilled out of a goodwill store."

"Cookie runs the kitchen. He has it the way he likes it."

"Jessie Lane." I swear Digby sighs as he says her name. The stars are in his eyes, and he gazes her with a look of complete and utter adoration.

I snort. She'll love it.

Jessie spins around to see him approaching from the living room.

"You must be Shane's friend. So you're not imaginary after all." She smiles an award-winning smile at him and holds out her hand for him to shake.

He takes it and raises it to his lips. "I think Shane's a bit too old for imaginary friends. I'm Digby."

I roll my eyes as Cookie and Ajax make their way in the back door.

"Here's the rest of the gang. Cookie, Ajax, this is Jessie."

Cookie lights up. "Good to meet you, Jessie. Shane says you've been having some issues. Welcome to our humble abode."

Ajax grunts.

Jessie extends her hand, but instead of shaking it, Cookie grabs her and pulls her into a hug. Panic fills her eyes, and I catch her gaze giving her a slow nod to try and let her to know she's safe.

"Sorry. I'll talk to him. He's a hugger," I mutter. "Ajax will make up for it by barely talking to you."

Ajax snickers.

"Is it just the four of you living here?" she asks.

I nod. "Yes. There's handful of farmhands, but they don't live on site. They're all signed to strict NDAs as my security work's spilled over onto the property before. So you don't have to worry about anyone sharing your location."

She offers up a thin-lipped smile. "You've had people staying here before?"

"No. But my office is here and while I try not to mix the two businesses, sometimes conversations at the worst times are unavoidable."

Digby grins. "He means he has to take calls even if he's cleaning up pig shit."

Jessie laughs. "I see."

"You'll learn all about it for yourself soon enough." I cross my arms.

"What are you talking about?" She cocks an eyebrow.

"These guys have been working without me the past few weeks, so tomorrow they sleep in while we take care of milking the cows."

She glares at me. "We're what?"

"Everyone on the farm contributes. If you're a good girl, Cookie will make you anything you want to eat."

Ajax snorts.

"I didn't realise working was a requirement of staying here," Jessie says.

My lips curl into a smile. "That's farm life. We all do our part."

She rolls her eyes. "Fine. Where's my room?"

Digby points toward the hallway off the living room. "Last room, right at the end. Next to Shane."

"Thanks," she grumbles as she walks away, and I shake my head.

"She trouble?" Ajax asks.

"She'll be fine. We just need to keep her busy and distracted."

"I hope you know what you're doing," Cookie says.

Letting out a sigh, I shake my head. "No idea. But whoever's been hassling her was way too close to where we were. I'm hoping putting a lot of distance between Jessie and her situation will keep her out of harm's way while they track this fucker down."

Cookie nods. "It all sounds awful. There's a lot of anger behind everything they've done."

I scrub my face with my hands. "There is. And I'm already seeing how she could have upset someone without even knowing it. I'm not sure what it is, but there's something buried deep inside her—something that causes her to be defensive and seem stand-offish. She's built a wall around her that's very, very hard to break through."

"Makes sense." He walks around the counter and flicks the button on the kettle. "I know she's famous, but it must have taken a lot of work for her to get to where she is. I'm sure that whole scene is cut-throat."

I walk to the other side of the kitchen counter and lean on my elbows. "From what I've seen, it is. But there also seems to be a lot of support."

"I'm glad she has you." His blue eyes pierce mine. "And now all of us. I was surprised when you asked us about bringing her home. It's not like you've ever done anything like that before. But now she's here, it makes a lot of sense."

"I know you guys won't hurt her. And my plan is to keep her working to help keep her mind off what's happening back in LA."

He shrugs. "Makes sense. Keep her attention focused. Whatever it takes."

I blow out a long breath. "Whatever it takes."

By seven in the morning, we've nearly finished the milking.

Ajax and Digby typically take turns managing the farmhands doing the work, but this morning it's me with Jessie.

"I hate you." Jessie glowers at me with tired eyes.

"I know. But we need to get this done. Then we'll go in and Cookie will make you whatever you want to eat."

She lets out a sigh. "I'm dreaming of the breakfast we had yesterday. Think he'll make me scrambled eggs and bacon?"

"He'll be really happy to."

"What on earth?" Jessie cries out.

A long streak of cow poop runs down her apron. Her nose wrinkles and her lips distort into a grimace. Her face is incandescent with rage.

"That's why we're wearing aprons, Jessie. Cows poop, like everything else on the planet."

Tears well in her eyes. "Why didn't you warn me?"

I frown. While I want her distracted, I don't want her to cry. Jesus. I think that would end me. Nothing deflates me faster than seeing her tears.

A dairy cow who's done what comes naturally has broken her rigidity.

"I'm sorry. How about you get that apron off and go get showered and changed?" I ask softly.

She shakes her head. "No. I said I'd do this and I meant it. I'll just be more careful next time."

I swallow hard. She's so stoic in the face of … everything. Whatever made her build those walls around her must be buried deep. She's not about to let anything shake her. Her temper might get the better of her at times, but there's so much more to Jessie Lane than tantrums and looking down her nose at people.

Footsteps behind us have her turning around.

"How's it going, Jessie girl?" Ajax asks.

A transformation comes over her, and I hold my breath at the way her whole face lights up at his greeting.

"So you do know how to talk?" She holds her head high.

He chuckles. "I don't like to waste words."

"Noted."

Casting his gaze over her, he shakes his head. "You got squirted on."

"Ewww. And yes." She laughs. I raise my eyebrows at her, and she shrugs before patting my chest. "Ajax isn't the one making me do this."

Ajax lets out choked laughter, his gaze shifting from Jessie to me and back again.

"I don't think anyone ever made you do anything in your life," I say.

Her face falls.

Fuck.

"Jessie. I didn't mean anything by that. I …"

Her beaming smile comes back, and she aims it straight at Ajax, ignoring me. "I think I'll get this apron off and get inside to shower. Walk with me?"

He glances between us again. "Sure."

A stabbing pain hits me in the chest as she walks away, led by the only man around here bigger than I am.

I want to distract her, not hurt her, and something tells me I said the wrong thing just then even though I don't know why.

Her confident swagger doesn't tell the whole Jessie Lane story.

And then there's the battle going on in my head over those shared moments we've experienced these past few days.

She's mine.

No. She's not.

Jessie Lane is a client.

But she's also stealing my heart.

15

A week later, I don't know what I was doing, agreeing to stay here.

My head hurts, I stink of cows and God knows what else, and the only thing I have to look forward to after milking is a long, hot shower.

Even then, I have to watch the amount of time I spend in there after using all the hot water the first three days I was here and ending up with four very cranky men.

They've done nothing for me to complain about, and they've all sworn to protect me, so getting them offside isn't a good idea.

And I do like them.

Digby is the one Shane took the selfie for, and he openly flirts with me no matter where we are or what we're doing.

Cookie keeps feeding me. The man makes mountains of food, but it all disappears. I guess that's what happens when you have not just the four men but a small group of farm workers to feed.

And then there's Ajax. Somehow, he's even bigger in stature than Shane. He tends to communicate with very few words and a mixture of grunts.

The best thing is, the issues back home are far from my mind. I have no doubt I'm being worked hard to distract me, and I resent the hell out of it, but at the same time I understand.

"Want a cookie, Jessie?" Cookie asks as I step inside the door.

I raise an eyebrow. "Is that some kind of trick question?"

He lets out a guffaw of laughter. "I made chocolate-chip cookies." Using a pair of tongs, he picks up a cookie and gives it to me. "They're still warm."

I pluck it from his grasp and take a bite, my eyes rolling back in my heard. "Oh my God, these are so good. it just melted in my mouth."

His wide smile lights up the whole kitchen. "That's what I was aiming for. But then, you're always easy to please."

"I have no problem being your guinea pig." Crumbs spray everywhere and I slap my hand over my mouth and laugh.

He waggles his eyebrows. "I love a woman with a good appetite."

"I'm going to have to work out extra hard when I go back to LA." I smile. "But it'll be worth it."

"I'll give you some more after your shower." He waves his hand in front of his nose.

I roll my eyes. "I'll take the hint."

Grumbling to myself, I head toward my room when I run straight into a wall.

A damp, solid, muscular wall.

Oh, God.

I put my hands in front of me to steady myself and strong arms grip mine as I drink in the sight of Shane in a towel.

Compared to him, the towel looks tiny.

My mouth goes dry.

The man is a mountain. His pecs are covered in hair that tapers off down that washboard stomach. Abs so sharply defined they could cut glass lead down to that happy trail from his belly button into the towel.

And that *V* on his hips ... I've seen a lot of shirtless men, but Shane puts most of them to shame.

I let out a contented sigh, and a chuckle shakes me out of my thoughts.

"My eyes are up here, your highness," Shane says.

Raising my gaze to his, I scowl at the laughter in his eyes. "I just wasn't expecting—"

"You're back early."

"Ajax felt sorry for me."

He snickers. "You got those guys wrapped around your little finger. Should have known."

"Not my fault they're a bunch of softies."

His dark eyes glisten. "And me?"

I gulp and press my hands against his pecs. "Nothing soft about you."

Catching my breath at the sight of his lips twitching into a smile, I pat his chest before taking a step back and walking around him.

As I scuttle the rest of the way to my room, his chuckle is the last thing I hear.

My heart pounds as I lean against the door and draw in some deep breaths.

I want Shane.

Not just because he's *the* hottest man I've ever seen and has no clue, but because he still sees me.

He always has.

And I see him.

16

JESSIE

Days turn into weeks.

Marcus still has people working on tracking my stalker, but there seem to be a lot of dead ends. There have been no more threats, but with me out of the picture, that's hardly surprising.

I'm kept busy doing odd jobs around the farm, and it takes my mind off it. I think that's one of the reasons Shane brought me here. It makes sense.

I know the routine by now, and it's my turn to hose down after the milking's done. I'm covered in cow poop again, and I must stink. I spray down the last of the floor and stand back.

How is Shane getting away with this? I'm paying for him to protect me, and I'm working for free. But I also can't say I'm hating it.

Shane's friends are the best. Having Cookie around is like having a gourmet chef on tap, and he's always eager to experiment with new things. At first, I marvelled at his metabolism because he eats as he cooks, but soon found the shed with the full gym not far from the house. Being able to get some miles on the treadmill has helped me get some endorphins from working out.

It also helps me push my increasing attraction to Shane to the back of my head.

I'm trying not to act like a pervert, but it's so tough. I skulk around the entrance to his bedroom when I know he's showering in the hope he'll come out wrapped in a towel.

No such luck.

But I also try and time my gym visits for when he's there. Watching him in a pair of gym shorts and a tank is almost as good as seeing him wrapped in a towel.

Almost.

For his part, he doesn't even seem aware of me as a woman, and for the first time in my life, lack of male attention is frustrating.

And always hovering in the background is the danger to me back home. While the life I've been living here keeps me busy, not a day passes when I don't wonder how long this will go on for and when I'll get my real life back.

The longer I'm out of the loop in Hollywood, the harder it'll be for me to climb my way back up. I've not had any work offers—things are really quiet on that front, and Marcus hasn't set up any auditions for me.

The arrival of spring brings warmer mornings. Not that keeping warm has been a problem since I arrived as I'm constantly on the go.

I almost look forward to the days when we start early and

the sun rises while the cows are milked. Dew covers the pastures, and there's that new season smell in the air.

"How's it going, Jessie girl?" Ajax asks as he walks into the shed, hands in pockets.

I drop the hose and slam my hands to my hips. "Great."

"I sense a bit of sarcasm in your answer." His lips quirk.

I'm still not sure about this guy. He seems solid and he must be because he's Shane's friend, but he's not as forthcoming as Digby or Cookie. Those two can talk until they're blue in the face—Cookie about cooking, Digby about movies.

Ajax, though, is still a mystery. He is indeed a man of few words, so they feel extra special when he uses them on me. And I try to make sure he knows how much I appreciate them.

"Sarcasm? Me? Never." I turn off the water and roll up the hose.

"I've got something to show you. Come with me."

My eyebrows rise. All I want right now is a hot shower and something to eat, but the smile on Ajax's lips has me curious.

Making my way across the room, I drop my apron into the hamper and tug off my gloves. "Where are we going?"

"Got a surprise for you in one of the sheds. If you're interested." He cocks his head.

I think this is the longest conversation I've ever had with him. "Lead on, McDuff."

He chuckles, and turns toward the door.

I walk, then run to catch up to his long strides. "So, what's the surprise?"

"If I told you, it wouldn't be a surprise. But have you seen my sheep?"

I look around as if I'm going to see one right in front of me. "I remember Shane saying there were a few."

He shrugs. "Only a handful. I wanted to raise one because I'm a big mutton fan." He licks his lips. "Nice mutton roast with gravy and roast potatoes. Can't beat it."

My stomach grumbles even though I'm not sure I've ever eaten mutton. "That's mature sheep, right?"

He nods. "Yep. But I didn't count on getting attached to these girls. Had them knocked up by some studly ram so we could get some lambs this year, and the first one's on its way."

I grasp his arm. "No."

"Ever watch a lamb being born?"

"I'm a city girl, Ajax. Where would I ever see anything like that?"

He grins. "You're in for a treat."

The shed he's leading me to is on the far side of the cow shed, farther than I've ever been on the farm.

Ajax opens a gate and leads me around to a wide open roller door. Inside, pens contain the half-dozen sheep, and I wrinkle my nose at the smell of hay and lanoline.

An older grey-haired man walks from pen to pen, checking on them. I shoot a curious look at Ajax.

"Our local vet. I want to make sure everything goes well."

"Do farmers usually have a vet with them?"

He shrugs. "Maybe not all the time, but these are my girls."

My heart leaps. Under all that gruffness is a heart of gold.

Ajax points to one corner. "She's close. So is the other one. It'll be a race to see who goes first."

His timing is immaculate.

We wander around before it becomes obvious something's happening with one of the sheep. I have no idea what to look for, but Ajax grasps my wrist and pulls my attention to it.

"Over here."

The vet's beside her as the sheep labours away.

I can't take my eyes off her, and when it finally happens, I clap my hands over my mouth. It's the grossest, most amazing thing I've ever seen as the lamb slides out.

Tears prick my eyes as I watch the mama sheep turn to lick her baby clean.

"It's something, huh?" Ajax asks softly.

"Amazing," I whisper.

Sniffing, I wipe my nose with my palm before leaning back on the fencing. Around me, Ajax and the vet busy themselves with the next sheep, but I stay watching this little baby until he stands on his wobbly legs.

"Takes your breath away, huh?" Shane's voice comes from behind me, and I turn to see the wonder in his eyes.

"I've never seen anything like it."

His hands touch the fencing on either side of me, and I'm engulfed by this huge man who surrounds me. The urge to lean back and into his arms is overwhelming.

Safe.

He sniffs. "Did Ajax bring you straight here from the cow shed?"

"How do you know?"

"Hate to tell you this, babe, but you really need a shower." He takes a step back, and I turn around and laugh at his screwed up face.

"This is your fault. Maybe I should just stay like this and hang around you."

Shane waves a hand over his nose. "Nah, I'm fine. I think I'll go inside if you're not."

I narrow my eyes. "Fine. But I'm coming back out afterwards because I want to see more."

He nods toward the next sheep. "Better make it fast because I don't think it'll be long before the next one's born."

With a backward glance, I run from the barn to the house.

Kicking off my boots, I push open the door. My stomach grumbles at the scents of tomato and herbs filling the kitchen.

"Jessie! I've been waiting for you to come in." Cookie claps his hands.

"You have?"

"I just made this new pasta sauce and I want an opinion."

I purse my lips. "Surely you could have got one of the others to try it?"

He shrugs. "I don't trust those Neanderthals."

I let out a laugh, and his eyebrows shoot up. "That was the first thing I called Shane."

"A word of love, I'm sure." He grabs a spoon from a drawer. "Here, try this." He dips the spoon in the pot and brings out the red sauce, offering it up to me.

I blow on the spoon before opening my mouth and moan as the sauce hits my tongue. I've got no idea what that mix of herbs is, but it's the best pasta sauce I've ever tasted.

"Good, huh?" His excited tone makes me smile. "I just watched Delaney Carter's new video and followed her recipe."

Delaney.

I swallow down the now bitter taste in my mouth, the well overdue apology she's owed springing to the surface of my mind.

"New video?" I haven't told Cookie about my connection to her. I've grown so close to everyone here that I'd hate to disappoint them. I wasn't aware that she had more videos, I've only seen the one she made with Reece.

"Yeah, she makes one about every month or so, and it's usually featuring ingredients I can get here." He tilts his head. "Don't go back to America. Stay with us," he says. "If I can't have her, I'll just keep you."

It takes everything in me not to roll my eyes at being second best yet again. "You could word that a little better."

His eyes widen. "Shit. Jessie. I didn't mean—"

"It doesn't matter. Your heart's in the right place." I lick my lips. "I hope dinner includes that sauce."

He nods. "Sure does. You came racing in here. Something going on?"

My eyes widen. "Lambs. Just gotta shower first."

I run to my room, grab some clothes, and head to the bathroom.

I'm not sure I've ever showered faster.

Shane laughs as I run across the paddock, my boots squelching in the grass.

"You're in for a treat." He smiles. "Twins."

My eyes widen, and I push my way into the shed with him on my heels.

"Just in time." Ajax beams.

One by one, the tiny wobbly-legged lambs come into the world.

I've seen a lot of things over the years. I've travelled the planet, sampled life in so many different countries, but today is right up there. It's one of the best days of my life.

I'm not sure how I came to be at this point in my life—or what I did to upset this person who's been threatening me. But I'm glad for it.

If it wasn't for Shane's actions, I'd be in LA, hiding myself away and feeling miserable. But out here, I feel more alive than I have in years.

How long until my bubble is burst?

17

———————

SHANE

I grit my teeth. "What do you mean, no leads?"

Marcus's tone is calm, and I have no idea how because this is dragging with no end in sight. I've kept Jessie distracted, but how long can this go on?

"I've got supposedly some of the best people on her case, but damn, Shane, this person's covered their tracks. The apartment building not having any security cameras really put a dent in things."

I chew on my bottom lip. "Did you contact Jessie's friends? The ones with the building code?"

"No."

I raise an eyebrow.

"I know them both well, Shane. Neither of them would hurt a hair on her head. Nor would they betray her trust."

"I'm not sure if I like that answer. So much for not leaving any stone unturned."

He sighs. "She's right about them. And besides, the one

thing the investigators have been able to tell me is that they think the person sending the threats is female. They've had a handwriting analyst working on the notes and the box."

Shaking my head, I puff out a breath. "At least that's something to work with."

"They've also pulled lists of all cast and crew from every production she's worked on from about a year before the letters started. That's hundreds if not thousands of people. So, there's a lot going on in the background."

"I can accept that."

Jessie wanders out of her room, yawning and scratching her head. As much as I'm trying to distract her, she distracts me as my thoughts wander.

I've seen her all made up for her movies, but without a shred of makeup and with bed hair, she's even more gorgeous.

"Where is everyone? I slept in." She stretches her arms above her head, her white tank rising and revealing a flat, tanned stomach. Her eyes widen as her gaze flicks from my face to my phone.

I hold up a finger. "Give me a moment."

She nods and heads into the kitchen.

"Jessie's up and I've got to go, but keep me posted," I say to Marcus quietly.

After disconnecting the call, I pause for a minute. I'm not sure how she's going to take this as things drag on, and while she's settled in here, at some point she's going to want to get on with her life.

Jessie emerges from the kitchen with a steaming mug of coffee. "What's going on?"

I drop onto the couch. She walks around it and sits beside me.

"Digby and Ajax are dealing with the milking this morning. We thought you could do with a sleep-in."

She scowls.

"I came in and turned off your alarm. The little snores you do in your sleep are so cute."

Jessie takes a sip of coffee. "I don't snore."

"Sure you don't."

She leans back. "There's something you're not telling me."

I play with my bottom lip between my teeth. "I spoke to Marcus. They're still at a loss as to who's responsible and—" I wondered if this might happen, so I've got a task for her today that'll hopefully completely distract her.

"Un fucking-believable." She shakes her head.

Despite trying to be serious, I chuckle. "You sound more and more like Digby every day." I nudge her knee. "I've got a special job for you today."

Her nostrils flare and she glares at me. "What?"

"The pigsty needs cleaning out. We all take turns."

Her jaw moves like she's chewing gravel. "Okay. Whatever."

Damn.

I almost expected her to throw a tantrum over it, and when she gets fiery about something—it does things to me it shouldn't.

"You won't be alone. One of the farmhands will be there to help and they know what to do."

It's a pretty big job, and it'll be time consuming.

I only hope it's enough to keep her mind off everything.

BY THE END of the day, I have regrets.

I think I took things too far today.

Jessie's been in the shower for at least an hour and I'm amazed there's any hot water left.

"Shane. What the fuck. Where's the hot water gone?" Cookie bellows from the kitchen.

Shit. Scratch that.

"Jessie cleaned out the pigsty."

He appears in the doorway and leans against the frame. "She did what?"

"It was her turn."

"Did you help her?"

I shake my head.

He smirks. "You're such a prick."

"She had help." I shrug.

"Yeah, but it's usually you and Ajax or Ajax and Digby. It's a massive job."

I blow out a long breath. "I spoke to Marcus this morning. They're still struggling to come up with leads in the case and she got really frustrated over it. She needed a big distraction. If she'd needed more help, I would have stepped in."

Cookie looks over my shoulder. "Good shower?"

I turn to see Jessie towelling her hair as she walks toward me.

I can't breathe.

She's wearing a pale green tank top, her nipples pressing

against the fabric. Yoga pants grace her long legs, hugging her slight curves. "Great shower. I think I used all the hot water, though. Cleaning up after the pigs is gross."

"Sounds like you drew the short end of the stick. Two of us usually do that job." Cookie ducks out of the room, calling over his shoulder. "I guess I'll wait for some more hot water."

Jessie stalks toward me. I've never seen her so enraged, with narrowed eyes and a sway in her hips that makes me ridiculously hard.

I can't help myself. It seems the angrier she gets, the more I want her. It's irrational, but I also know that today I have a lot to atone for because what I did wasn't fair to her in the slightest.

"Today was the worst day since I got here, and I didn't even mind it because you've all been so good to me, but you lied." She slams her hands to her hips.

"I know."

"I hate you." She pounds on my chest, her green eyes flashing in anger.

"I know."

Sexual tension thrums in the air between us. Her chest rises and falls rapidly, and her focus falls to my lips.

"I hate you, but you make me feel things no one else does."

She slows, meeting my gaze. I've never been harder than I am right now, drinking in the sight of her rage.

"I know," I say softly.

My words defuse the situation, and she tosses a curl of that red hair over her shoulder before stamping her feet all the way back to her room. The frame rattles as she slams the door.

I can't do this.

I can't have her in my house.

But I can't let her go.

She's safer here right now than anywhere else, and I'm selfish. I don't want her to *be* anywhere else.

Jessie Lane is a barb right in the heart. I hate my feelings and love them all at the same time. I want her, but I can't …

I run my fingers through my hair and stay in one spot, glued to the floor.

The handle turns and her long fingers curl around the door, pulling it until it's wide open and she's standing, glaring at me.

Without a word, she runs, launching herself into my arms. My heart thuds. This shouldn't happen, but since the day I met her, I knew Jessie Lane would be a weakness.

"Don't you do this unless you mean it," I murmur.

"I still hate you." Her lips crash onto mine, and I grasp her around the waist. She lets out a whimper as our tongues touch.

This isn't supposed to happen.

I don't do this with clients.

But my want and need for her is so great, it overrides any common sense.

"My room or yours?" I mumble against her lips. "My bed's better."

"Yours."

I lift her up and she lets out a whoop. Cookie sticks his

head out of his room and just shakes his head as I pass him in the hallway, carrying my prize triumphantly.

Everything else in the world disappears when we enter my room and close the door. I deposit her on the bed and tug at her yoga pants. She struggles to push herself up, then grabs for my shirt.

"One thing at a time, woman."

"Hurry up."

I push her back down and pull her pants off.

She laughs at the sound of the delicate fabric tearing. "Those are my four hundred-dollar La Perla panties."

"I'll take out a mortgage to pay for them." I hold up the material. "Are you sure these are even classed as panties? It's more like a tiny scrap."

Jessie pushes herself back up and snatches them out of my hand. "A girl's gotta have some luxury when she's been cleaning out pig poop all day."

I purse my lips. "Point taken. Maybe I should reward you for having to do that terrible job."

She rests back on her elbows. "And how are you going to do that, Mr Johnson?"

I run my gaze over her, and she shivers. "Well first, I thought I'd eat your pussy."

Jessie shakes her head. "No time for that. I want you inside me."

"You're so bossy, Ms Lane."

"I'm on the pill, and I don't think I can have children anyway. Just fuck me," she begs.

"Jessie."

She pushes herself into a seated position. "Don't mess

this up, Shane. I've been thinking about this since the day I ran into you coming out of the shower." Lowering her head, she looks at me from under her eyelashes. "I just thought a lot about that while *I* was in the shower."

Holy shit.

I drop my pants and fist my cock.

She leans forward. "I'm ready. I can see you are. What's the hold up?"

"Come here."

She rolls off the bed.

I sit on the edge of it and beckon her with my index finger. A smile spreads across her lips and she swaggers toward me.

God, she's beautiful. Her full breasts tipped with peach-coloured nipples beg for me to take them into my mouth. She's thin, but my hands itch to grip her curvy hips while she rides me.

She stands right in front of me.

"You sure you want this?" I ask.

Jessie takes my hand and guides it to her bare pussy. I slide a finger into her slick folds.

"You're so wet," I whisper.

"I touched myself in the shower thinking about you."

My heart races, and I pull her toward me until she straddles my legs. Her pussy's inches from my cock, her heat burning my thighs.

"Fuck me," she whispers.

She pushes up when I hold my cock to her entrance before slowly lowering herself onto it. I swallow hard as she raises slightly before dropping down again.

"Slow. I want this to last," I say.

Gripping her hips, I lean forward and take one of her nipples into my mouth. Her coconut-scented skin is soft, and she gasps when I suck gently.

She bounces up and down on my cock, my hands guiding her while I place kisses on her breasts.

"It's not hard enough. I need it harder," she grumbles.

"You got it." I help her down off me. "Crawl up onto the bed. On your hands and knees."

As soon as she reaches the pillows, she wiggles her arse in the air. "Hurry up."

She gasps when I crawl up behind her, slide inside her, and then grasp her breasts. I throw my head back, pounding her pussy.

This isn't enough.

I want more.

But that will have to wait until next time because right now, she's letting out moans so loud, our neighbours can probably hear her. And they live at least two kilometres away.

"Shane," she groans.

"This is just round one, sweet. I'm going to keep you so tied up with me that you forget your own name."

"I already forgot. Keep going."

I run my hands up her stomach and grip her breasts. "So demanding, woman."

Jessie laughs, her hot pussy squeezing me tight.

"You're going to be the death of me." I pinch her nipples and move my hands back to her hips.

"I hope not because once isn't going to be enough," she pants.

Fuck.

She's driven me crazy, but I want her more than I've ever wanted anything or anyone in my whole life. Jessie owns me in a way no woman ever has.

"You're in my bed now. Good luck ever getting out of it." My body tightens and I can't hold off anymore. My release hits me so hard, I let out a loud grunt.

Jessie's laughter squeezes every last drop out of me, and after a moment, I pull out of her, dropping onto the bed.

"And you thought I was some precious princess." She drops her head and runs her tongue around one of my nipples.

"You called me a Neanderthal."

Her cheeks flush again. "You're a Neanderthal who knows how to fuck."

I slide a hand in her hair and pull her to me for a kiss. "Thanks, but I thought you'd know this is a much bigger deal for me than just a fuck."

She blinks rapidly. "For me too."

"So, I'll take it as a compliment, but ..."

Jessie sucks on her bottom lip. "I suck at relationships."

"Yeah? Me too."

She smiles. "I guess we're as bad as each other?"

I push a lock of auburn hair behind her ear. "I guess so. But I want to try. I don't want this to be a one and done thing."

Her smile widens. "Me neither."

I kiss her softly. "Quick shower and round two?"

"Didn't Cookie want the hot water next?"

Grinning, I run my hand down her back. "He can wait."

18

JESSIE

I don't know when I last had a boyfriend.

Not just someone to spend the occasional night with. I've had plenty of those over the years.

But someone who wanted to try more.

Shane's seen me at my worst and still wants to be with me. Sure, I'm paying him to be here, but he's my rock. I trust him more than I trust anyone else at this point.

And now he's being so gentle—I didn't know he had it in him. His tender caresses and kisses are the opposite of the pounding I wanted before. His calloused hands make their way over my naked body, and I melt at his touch.

"Perfect," he whispers.

We're not long out of the shower, but my body's slicked with sweat just from the frantic kissing and touching going on.

Shane's hand's between my legs, and I let out a sigh as he

runs his tongue up my neck. Tension pools in the base of my stomach. I'm so close.

I close my eyes.

I'm a big fan of sex. I love it. But when I reach this point, I'm taken back to my past and shame floods through my system, doing its best to kill my arousal.

It's so rare for a man to make me come, but I want that with Shane so badly.

"Give it to me, Jessie," he murmurs, laying gentle kisses on my collarbone.

His large fingers are magic as sensation courses through my veins.

Please.

I plead with myself.

I can't do it.

Tears prick my eyes. I'm not sure why, but I thought being with Shane would be different. If I have sex for the sake of having sex, I fake it. There have been times when I've been close, but I never quite make it.

By myself, it's not a problem.

With a man?

There's only one thing to do—I let out a moan and shudder just like I do on screen.

An award-winning performance if I do say so myself.

He stops, raising his head and fixing his dark gaze on me. "Did you just ... fake it?"

My eyebrows rise. I've faked it with every man I've ever been with. No one's ever called me out. "What? Why ...?"

"You think I'm not going to notice when the sounds

you're making don't match what your body's doing?" His eyes search mine.

I shrug. "No one ever has before."

Shane frowns. "What do you mean?"

"I mean ..." I run my finger down his arm. "I've always faked it. Guess I'm not as good an actress as I thought I was."

He captures his hand in mine. "You seemed really into it."

I blink rapidly. "I am. It's just ..." I hold my breath. Could I really trust him with the truth? Shane's changed my life in more ways than he could ever know, but can I risk whatever this is between us before it's even really started?

What if he's repulsed by my past? What if he thinks I'm the one who caused it?

My stomach flips.

"Jessie. Tell me what's wrong." He shifts, pulling me into his arms until I'm on my side, pressed against him, my head resting on his chest.

I want this to be more. I want this to be real. If I don't have faith in him, then this whole thing is pointless.

"I don't want you to think any less of me," I whisper.

He kisses the top of my head. "There's nothing you can say that will make me feel that way."

I draw in a deep breath, raise my head, and meet his gaze. "I was fifteen when it started."

His intense stare almost makes me recoil. But he's on my side. I have to remember that.

"My mother was the one with all the ambition. I was just the kid who wanted to act, and she found some guy who promised her the world. He was going to manage my career and make me a star."

I stroke Shane's arm. The action gives me comfort.

"It took a while, and a few auditions, but I landed a commercial on a local TV station." I shake my head. "My parents were fighting. Dad was good at losing himself in a bottle of whiskey. I remember that day because he pushed Mom over whether this was what I wanted or what she wanted. He let her walk all over him, and she drove me to my manager's office."

Shane's grasp on me tightens. I can't look him in the face —the shame is too great.

"He asked if he could see me alone. He wanted to spend some time coaching me on how to handle myself on the set or some other excuse. My mother told me to be a good girl and do whatever he told me."

"Jesus." Shane grips my chin and guides my gaze back to his. "Are you telling me what I think you are?"

Tears roll down my cheeks, and I nod. "That was just the first time."

His jaw clenches.

"I think I struggle when I'm with men because I didn't know any better back then. He made me ..."

Shane nods. "What was his name?"

"Does it matter now?"

"It will matter when I end him."

I blink, my eyes fixed on him. "You're not disgusted by me?"

"Why would I be disgusted by you? You were a kid. He was a grown-arse man. And your mother? What the hell was she thinking?"

Tears blur my vision. All this time, I've never confided in

anyone for fear of them not believing me or thinking my actions put me in the wrong.

Shane believes me.

He has faith in me.

"His actions are still causing you problems, Jessie. The guy needs to be strung up, and you need to know that it's okay to let go. You're not at fault in any way."

I bury my face in his chest and weep. He's right, and I think I've known it for some time. I've felt a lot of guilt and shame over the years, and maybe all I needed was someone to just take my side.

My mother never did.

My father wanted to sweep it under the carpet.

"Did you ever see a therapist about this? Talk to anyone?" The anguish in his voice makes me want to cry more.

I shake my head. "No. I just wanted to move on."

"Oh, Jessie." He wraps his arms around me tight and kisses my hair. "None of this is on you, baby. We'll find you someone to talk this through."

My heart leaps. *We.*

"There's more," I whisper.

"Tell me."

"It wasn't just him. Later on, he'd take me away for weekends for photo shoots, but the man doing them was a friend of his, and some of them were nudes." I let out a sob. "And then he'd make me have sex with the photographer."

Shane draws in a deep breath. "You know I'm gonna want names."

"I don't even know what his friend's last name was, but I've been terrified for years that some of those photos would resurface somewhere. Some of those weekends are so vague because they'd drug me first. So I don't even know …"

"And no one got you help?"

"No." My voice is so small. "Eventually, my dad sobered up and took control of the situation. He still doesn't know everything—he didn't want to know. He just wanted it to stop. Mom threatened to leave with me, but Dad told her he'd take it all to the authorities, so Mom left. Dad paid for me to do the acting course I always wanted, and from there I established my career and left the past behind."

Shane runs one hand down my spine. I breathe slowly, trying to regain some kind of equilibrium. His touch soothes and calms me. He's just so easy to be with.

Is this what it was like for Josh when he met Delaney, or Reece when he met Pania? Shane's just the right fit—he's right for me.

"You didn't leave the past behind though. It's right in here." Shane lifts his hand from my back and taps my forehead. "You gotta get on top of that because it must be eating you alive."

"How?"

"Did telling me help?"

I nod.

"Then, that's a start. Do you trust me?"

"Literally with my life."

His lips curl into a smile. "There is nothing you can do or say that's going to put me off this thing with you. I hope you know that."

I nod.

"Good, because I'm going to kiss the fuck out of you and

then we're going to start again. And this time, I'll keep talking to you and telling you what I hope you need to hear so you can come with me."

My eyes widen. "I don't know ..."

"Don't ever try faking it with me. I. Will. Know."

That warm feeling in my chest grows. He wants me just as I am, and I don't have to pretend anymore. I can just be me.

"There's something else I should tell you," I say.

His eyes—his eyes are so full of pain. He's taken everything I've given him and accepted it, but will there be a breaking point?

He presses his forehead to mine and strokes my hair. "I'm right here. Whatever you have to tell me."

"The reason ... the reason I don't think I can have children was that after all that, I got really sick. Dad took me to the doctor and I had an infection that should have been dealt with a lot earlier. The doctors think it might have left me infertile. Not that we're at that stage of our relationship, or that you ever might want to have kids with me. Or that—"

Shane kisses me softly. "We'll cross that bridge if we ever come to it."

"I just feel better telling you everything," I whisper.

"Then I'm honoured you trust me with it."

I let out a sigh of relief. "I always felt like people would judge me. Even my friends."

"If anyone judges you for any of that, they're not your friends." He kisses me again, and I melt into him. "Now I think I'm just going to hold you for a while—until you're really ready to try this again."

My heart leaps. I should have had faith that he'd be on my side. "What do I get if I come?"

He grins. "Promise I'll eat your pussy any time you want me to."

I purse my lips. "You haven't done it yet, so I don't know if that's a reward."

His mouth falls open. "Are you doubting my ability?"

"We might have to try it a few times to see just how good you are." I shrug, and his eyes darken as a smirk crosses his lips.

"Only one way to find out."

AFTER A FULL-BODY MASSAGE, Shane turns on the television and messes around on Netflix.

"I thought we were ..." I furrow my brow.

He taps the remote against his cheek. "We are. I'm just working on relaxing you first. We seem to have skipped a few steps in our relationship."

I raise my eyebrows. "We have?"

"I thought a bit of Netflix and chill might help. You know, even though you told me you weren't that kind of girl." His grin lights up his whole face, and I can't help but laugh.

"I'm totally that kind of girl. Especially with you."

He scrolls through the movies while I snuggle up against him. "Glad to hear it."

"What are we watching?"

Shane's nose wrinkles. "I'm not sure. I wish your movie

was out already. Then I could lie here and watch you on that pole."

I laugh. "I hate watching myself on screen."

"Then I guess one of your movies is out of the question?"

I look up at the television and cringe as he stops at *Twisted Hearts*. That's the movie I made with Josh a few years ago—the shoot that led him back to Delaney. "Not that one."

He studies me for a moment and then scrolls on until he finds *Die Hard*. "That's more like it."

"I've never seen it," I say.

His mouth falls open. "You're kidding."

"No." I shrug.

"You're in for a treat."

"I'm hoping I'll be busy doing other things."

He clicks start and nestles into the pillows.

For a moment, I gaze at him before looking back toward the TV.

Guess he's serious.

About twenty minutes into the movie, I'm beginning to think he's changed his mind when his hand brushes up my inner thigh and he parts my legs.

"Shane?" I whisper.

"Ignore me." He slides two fingers inside me.

"I'm not sure I can ignore you."

He laughs against my neck before kissing it softly. Sliding his fingers back over my clit, he repeats the action slowly and my hips rise to meet him.

"Are we even watching this movie anymore?" I ask.

He nibbles on my earlobe. "I'm not watching the movie. I'm watching you."

My eyelashes flutter. "Me?"

"I want to see you the moment I make you come."

He arches his fingers back over my clit, and I draw in a sharp breath. "Oh."

I fight the urge to close my eyes, and I bury my face in his neck, sucking hard.

"It's been years since I had a hickey." He chuckles. His hand slows, his gentle strokes taking me back to that feeling of being on the edge again.

"I'm just marking you as mine."

He slides his fingers into me. "You're so fucking beautiful, Jessie. Give yourself to me. Be mine."

I raise my head and meet his raw gaze. His eyes search my own as he pumps his fingers in and out and over my clit. My eyelids are so heavy, and I fight the urge to close them.

"Keep your eyes on mine. Give me what I want."

"I want you." I raise my hand to cup his cheek.

His intense gaze makes my heart pound.

"I want you too. And once you've come, I'll spend the rest of the night inside this hot, tight pussy."

My breath hitches. Tension pools in my stomach again. We were together earlier tonight, but not like this. He was clearly paying attention earlier, but this time, his eyes are still on mine, and I can't see anything else but him.

"Shane," I cry out.

"That's it. Give it to me." He plants kisses under my ear. His hot breath on my skin brings me closer. My eyes want so desperately to close.

"I see you, Jessie Lane. I've always seen you," he

murmurs. "You're my North Star—the brightest light in my sky. When I'm with you no one else exists."

Gripping his arm, I take shallow breaths, my eyes finally winning the battle and closing.

My whole world explodes. Wave after wave of pleasure hits me, and I sink into the mattress, boneless and spent.

"That's my girl." His mouth is on mine in an instant, and tears prick my eyes as his deep kiss makes my head swim.

I'm still shaking when he positions himself between my legs and plunges his tongue into my pussy.

"Shane," I call out.

His laughter's muffled against me, and I move my hips to meet his tongue.

I throw my head back when his hands clamp onto my breasts, teasing my nipples as he sucks gently on my clit.

I'm his.

He's mine.

I've always enjoyed sex, but I had no idea it could be this good. And it's all because he took the time to see me. That wasn't just a line. He meant it.

"I need to be inside you," he says.

"Please."

As he rises above me, I place a hand on his chest. His eyes, his eyes are so full of an emotion I don't recognise. Is this love?

He slides into me, and I raise my knees to give him deeper access.

"I could die happy, buried in your pussy," he says.

I laugh, and he lets out a moan.

Closing my eyes, I sigh contentedly as I meet each of his

thrusts with my own, and he buries his face in my neck, kissing, licking, and whispering words that make me blush.

Behind him, the television flickers, forgotten, and I guess I can say I still haven't seen the movie.

Shane fills me, fulfils me, takes me to the brink again before it's his turn, his lips parting as he groans his release, pulsing inside me.

His weight settles on me, his expression so blissful it makes my throat tighten.

"Never going to get enough of you," he murmurs. His eyes flicker open, and he fixes his gaze on mine.

"I feel the same way, big man." I slide my arms around his neck. He shifts, and I pull him back down. "Not so fast."

"My weight on you—"

"Is just fine. I just want you close."

He drops his head and nuzzles my neck before rolling off me. "Come here, then."

I could almost purr, wrapped in his embrace. "Why? Why did you do this for me?"

He cups my face and presses a gentle kiss to my lips. "Because you're worth it—you're worth everything."

Tears prick my eyes.

"I tried so hard not to cross the line between us, but it's an impossible fight, Jessie. You're in so deep that I wouldn't know how to get you out if I tried. And I don't want to try."

I bury my face in his chest. "I'm sorry if I was difficult when we first met. We should have stayed in a hotel."

He kisses the top of my head. "I'm sorry I put you to work when we got here. You don't have to."

I laugh against his chest. "I think I figured that out early on." Raising my head, I meet his bemused gaze. "But I've enjoyed being here far more than I ever thought I would."

"No more pigs. I promise."

Reaching over, I grasp his arm and squeeze. "Thank God."

His torso rumbles with laughter and I close my eyes. Sleeping won't be an issue tonight. I'm safer than I've ever been, in more ways than one.

And I'm falling in love.

19

JESSIE

No one says a word when I move my things into Shane's room.

It's like they all had an expectation that this would happen. I guess we weren't as discreet as we thought we were in our mutual attraction.

Although, now that attraction threatens to consume us both as we can't get enough of each other.

I no longer have to get up for early morning starts. The other men are on duty and Shane and I have the house to ourselves, which is just as well because every time we're together, intimacy gets a little easier between us.

I think I love Shane.

I've always found it so hard to connect with people, but there's a connection between Shane and I that's on a whole other level.

Is that love?

We have a level of trust that goes deep. So deep that I can

only assume that this is what love is. He hasn't let me down yet.

I joke about him having magical fingers, but the reality is that he listens and he pays attention to me. Maybe that's all I ever needed.

Shane puts my needs first, physically and emotionally, and while I've had other lovers who claim to have done the same, I've come to realise no one really has. Until now.

"Is this what therapy is like?" It's late at night. I'm hazy from orgasming and curled around Shane's naked body.

Chuckling, he plants a kiss on my forehead. "I still think you should look into actual therapy. Not that I'm complaining."

An almighty crash of saucepans comes from the kitchen.

Shane shoots off the bed.

He turns, raising one finger to his lips, and I nod.

"I'm going to check that out. You okay?" he whispers.

I nod. "Want me to hide in the wardrobe?"

His lips twitch. "If you want to, sweetheart. But I think you'd be better off going into the en suite and locking the door."

I cover my mouth with my hand as I giggle.

"Be back as soon as I find out what that was."

Shouting comes from outside, but I can't make out the voices. Has my stalker found me here? I dart into the bathroom, throwing the lock shut. Setting down the toilet lid, I take a seat, close my eyes, and take deep breaths.

Please be nothing. Please be nothing. Please be nothing.

The silence gets to me.

Is Shane okay?

What about the others?

Did I bring this to them?"

Laughter outside the door makes me open my eyes.

"Jessie. You can come out now." Shane taps on the door. "Ajax and Digby are back from the pub and Ajax is pissed."

"If he's angry, why should I come out?" I curl up into ball.

He laughs. "No, sweetheart. He's drunk. Walked straight into Cookie's pans hanging in the kitchen. After he bumped his head on the back door. That was the noise."

I stretch my legs out before pushing myself to my feet. "So, it's safe?"

"The only thing to worry about out here is the seven-foot man sighing because he's in love."

Unlocking the door, I open it.

Shane holds out a hand and I take it. "Come and see for yourself," he says.

Cookie's standing in the middle of the kitchen, his hands on his hips. It's hard to ignore that he's half-naked, his pyjama pants sitting low on his hips. I'm not sure how he eats so much and looks like that, but he's as cut as Shane is.

"What the fuck, Ajax? You've probably dented my good pans," Cookie says.

"Shouldn't have left them hanging on the ceiling, then. They were in my way." The words are slurred.

I clamp my lips together to stop myself from laughing. Ajax turns and sees me, his lips curling into a breathtaking smile.

The giant of a man wraps his arms around me and pulls me in tight against his side, kissing the top of my head. I've got no choice but to let him do it, despite him smelling like a brewery. He guides us to the couch and pulls me down next to him.

"I'm sorry if I scared you, Jessie girl. I just had a bit too much to drink."

Shane snorts.

"But I think I met the love of my life tonight, so I'm floating on a cloud."

I shoot an amused glance at Shane.

Patting Ajax's chest, I gaze up at him. "That's great, big guy. How about you get some sleep now?"

"Wait." Digby rounds the couch, carrying a large glass of water and some pills. "Take this before you go to sleep."

"I'm not sure there's enough water in the world to stop him from getting a hangover," Shane mutters.

"Imagine how much beer it took to get him drunk." Digby shakes his head as Ajax does as he's told.

"I'm gonna sit here and talk to Jessie. She's a woman. She'll know how I can win my woman's heart." He winks.

I snicker. "It'll be easier when you're sober. Get some sleep, Ajax, and we'll work out a plan of action tomorrow."

He places another kiss in my hair, chuckling as Shane growls. "Thank you. Does this place good to have the female touch around it. Don't you ever go anywhere."

I pat his arm. "I'm not going anywhere anytime soon from the looks of things." *I'm not even currently sure how I'm getting off this couch.*

"I'm glad to hear that." He frowns. "Though I wish they'd catch this dickhead threatening you. If I found him, I'd—"

"I don't think we need to hear your violent fantasies,"

Shane says, holding out a hand for me to take. "Come on. Let's go back to bed."

Ajax lets me go, patting me on the behind as I stand to take Shane's hand. Shane just shakes his head and pulls me closer before leading me to the bedroom and closing the door.

"Is he going to be okay?" I ask.

"Eventually." Shane tugs me toward the bed, and I climb in beside him. "He'll probably fall asleep on the couch, wake up on the floor, and be grumpy as fuck in the morning."

"He seemed happy." I snuggle into Shane's arms, resting my head on his chest.

Shane strokes my arm. "He did. Must be something special about this woman. Ajax tends to keep that kind of thing close to his chest. I've never seen him react like that before."

I yawn. "I'll get the whole story tomorrow."

"If anyone can, it'll be you. He's got a real soft spot for his Jessie girl."

I nuzzle Shane's chest. "He's such a sweetheart. So are the others. I'm so glad you brought me here."

"Me too, sweet. Me too."

AJAX SNORES.

There's nothing dainty about it as he lies on the floor, his arms stretched out at his sides, and snuffles and snorts.

"Told you," Shane murmurs. "I'm going out to help with

the cows. Make him a coffee when he wakes up. Painkillers are in the third drawer down at the end of the bench."

I lean against him. "Will do."

He pecks me on the lips. "Go back to bed for a while. It's cold."

Turning, I look over my shoulder. "Come and snuggle with me."

He laughs and points at the floor. "*That* is why I can't. I'll be back in a few hours and using you to warm myself up."

I roll my eyes. "Good to know I'm useful for that."

"There are a lot of things you're useful for, Jessie. That's just one of them." Shane nods toward Ajax. "He owes me big time for this."

I snort and give his arm a shove. "Sooner you get this done, the sooner you can join me back in bed."

With another quick kiss, he disappears out the door. I take another look at Ajax, shake my head, grab a blanket from the back of the couch, and spread it over him before I make my way back to bed with a yawn. The sheets are still warm and Shane's scent is everywhere. I snuggle into his pillow and close my eyes. Sleep's easy to come by.

I'm not sure how long I sleep, but the sun's peeping through the windows when I wake.

Shane's not back.

It's not unusual. It only takes one small thing to go wrong for his return to be delayed.

My stomach rumbles, and I pat it.

I slide out of bed and slip on a bra before tugging on a T-shirt and pulling on some sweatpants.

The house is quiet as I make my way into the living room.

Ajax's large body still occupies the space in front of the couch, but at least he's sitting up. He gives me a rueful smile.

"You okay?" I ask. "I'll make some coffee."

"Just a big old headache." He chuckles. "Guess I caused an uproar."

I snicker. "You could say that."

"That's not me, Jessie girl. I'm not the type of guy who goes out and gets messy. But we had a great night out."

He pulls himself up onto the couch, and I squeeze his shoulder. "Coffee and painkillers coming right up. And a large glass of water."

"Thank you." He grabs hold of my hand. I swallow hard but don't pull back. I might be crazy about Shane, but all these men are important to me now. They've welcomed me into their home and treated me like a friend. There's no tiptoeing around why I'm here, but they've accepted me and I'm one of them now.

I pull my hand away and pat the back of his. "You're welcome. I could do with some coffee myself."

By the time I've made the coffee, Ajax is leaning back against the couch. He's so tall his neck almost drapes over the back of it, his head at an unnatural angle.

"Here. These first," I hold out a glass of water and two small white pills.

After popping the pills, he drains the glass before swapping it for a large mug of coffee.

He takes a deep breath of the coffee steam and sighs. "I haven't done that in a long, long time. But we had so much fun."

I smile, taking a seat next to him. "Sounds like it. Tell me about her."

He shrugs. "We just met. But she's something special. Women don't usually look twice at me."

I run my gaze over him. Ajax is a big guy. His hair is cut short but not clipped army-style like Digby, and his features are weathered but handsome. He has visible scars, and a couple of them are facial, so I can see why some people might be intimidated by it.

We haven't known each other long, but this guy has a heart of gold. He deserves all the happiness he can get.

I rub his arm. "Good for you."

He studies me closely. "I'm going to ask Shane if I can bring her for dinner or something. I know he's got us on tight restrictions when it comes to who comes and goes, but ..."

"I'll put in a good word."

"She's not from around here. Came down from Auckland a few weeks ago for a change of pace. And she's got a twinge of Australian in her accent, so I think she was there for a while."

I nod. "I'm looking forward to meeting her."

His whole face lights up in a smile. "Can't wait for that, Jessie girl. I'd like your approval."

Laughing, I shake my head. "You don't need it."

"I meant what I said last night. Having you around has been great. I think we all forget what it's like to be around women with all the hours we do here." He takes a sip of his coffee. "Plus, you make great coffee."

Laughing, I shake my head. "That machine means it's pretty foolproof."

He wrinkles his nose. "It just confuses me. Give me instant anytime." His sheepish look makes me laugh. "Except for this. I like this."

"I think this is the most you've ever said to me." I tilt my head.

"I'm not good with new people. That's why last night was so surprising. I struck up this conversation with Victoria and didn't want the night to end."

Lifting my hand, I squeeze his forearm. "She sounds great."

"It's a small community here. Not many opportunities to meet women. And you're taken."

I slap his hand. "You're too cute."

He drinks deep and lets out a sigh. "If it's okay with Shane, I'll invite her for dinner on Saturday."

I nod. "I like it. That gives us three days to work on him."

"You'd do this for me?" His puppy-dog eyes are making my heart melt, and I rub his arm in response.

"The four of you welcomed me into your home. The least I can do is help you get laid."

He guffaws. "I'm not sure it'll go that far, but I appreciate the support."

I stand, patting him on the shoulder. "Let me get you some more water. That's what's going to make you feel better."

AFTER BREAKFAST, Shane goes out with Cookie and Digby to

deal with other tasks around the farm. When Ajax goes for a nap, I've got the house to myself for the first time.

I've not thought about the situation back home for a while, and there's been no word from Marcus.

Not that I've spoken to him about this. I've left Shane to deal with it.

I'm so settled here, I barely miss home. I've not had this much time off in years. There's always been something on the go, and while I usually get restless while on vacation, this trip is different.

There's a lot I need to catch Marcus up on anyway.

Grabbing my phone, I dial Marcus, closing my eyes as the line rings. He's so good at answering my calls, but has he just forgotten about me out here?

"Jessie." The warmth in his greeting makes me smile.

"Hey, Marcus. It's been a while."

"It has. Shane and I have been checking in with each other, so I know you've been busy."

I laugh. "You don't know the half of it."

"You sound okay."

I flop onto the couch. "I *am* okay. I wish this whole thing was over, but I'm not hating it here. How's the investigation going?"

He lets out a sigh that tells me all I need to know before he says it. "Slowly. They're still trawling through everyone who could have been on that set and that's taking a while. There's a group who haven't been contactable and we need to eliminate everyone. Having you in that apartment building with no cameras wasn't the best move."

Swallowing hard, I pick at the hem of my T-shirt. "It'll teach me for being cheap."

"How are things going there?" he asks.

"Well ..." I lick my lips. "Shane and I ... we're ..."

Marcus is silent.

"We're sharing a room."

It takes a moment for him to speak. "I see."

It's hard to gauge his reaction; his tone's so neutral.

"Are you happy, Jessie?"

I fight a smile, but it's impossible to stop. "Very."

"Then that's all that matters."

Tears prick my eyes. This is the closest thing I'll get to a father's approval, and my heart's so full right now.

"Shane's a good man. It bothers me that he's clearly crossed that professional line, but it's been a long time since you've been truly happy, Jessie, and if you are, that means more to me than anything."

I sniff. "I am. I'm so glad we came here. It's been good for me."

"Maybe this is what you needed—albeit without the stress of these threats hanging over you. A decent break and a decent man."

Laughing, I nod. "I think you're right."

"It's good to hear that laugh." He puffs out a breath. "I've got to get going for a meeting, but I miss you, kiddo. Stay safe and let's hope you're home sooner rather than later."

"Thank you." I grip the phone and look up as something moves at the end of the couch. Shane takes a seat.

"I'll talk to you later. Give my regards to Shane, and he'd better take extra good care of you now," Marcus says.

"I will."

I draw a deep breath as I disconnect the call and meet Shane's gaze. "Marcus," I say, nodding to my mobile.

He nods. "Thought it might be. How is he?"

"I told him about us."

His expression is blank, and I frown.

"I kind of left that out of our conversations," he says. "I didn't want him to think—"

"Think we were together?" I ask.

His brows knit. "No. Shit. That's not what I meant. It's just ... I am being paid to keep you safe. Hooking up with you isn't part of the job description."

I scrub my face with my palm. "That just makes it sound like—"

He's across my side of the couch in an instant, grasping my arms. "I'm trying not to say anything I don't mean. You and me, it's got nothing to do with the job. It's just that Marcus might not see it that way."

I blink rapidly and look away. "He was actually really good about it. Not impressed that we've crossed that line, but he thinks you might be good for me."

Shane grips my chin and turns my head so I can't do anything but look into his eyes. "I don't care what he thinks about *us,* but I know you do."

I nod. "You know my story. Marcus has always been there in a way my parents never were. Having his approval is important to me."

"Then, I'll talk to him about us next time we speak and make sure he knows how I feel about you." He lets go of my chin and kisses me softly. "I'm sorry I didn't get back inside to climb into bed with you. Tonight, we'll go to bed early."

"Sounds good to me."

He sighs. "I've got to help Cookie put up some of the new shelving we bought, so I'm in to grab a quick lunch and back to it. Come with me if you want to, or have some time for yourself. I doubt Ajax will be around until dinnertime."

Laughing, I rest my head on his shoulder. "I forced some liquids into him earlier. Pretty sure he'll be sleeping it off the rest of the day. I think I'm just going to lounge around here, maybe find something to watch on TV."

Shane kisses my temple. "Use the computer in my bedroom if you want to use the net. My laptop is locked, but the desktop isn't."

"I have missed my Hollywood gossip."

He chuckles. "I bet. Let's grab some lunch."

Surfing the Internet turns out to be the thing that makes me homesick.

Josh and Reece are working on a new movie. I'm not sure what the exact details are, but there's a hole in my heart over not being able to work with them. They're producing this time, not starring, but I'd kill just to be involved. When I get home ... well, there are some amends I need to make.

Declan's night out in Vegas turned out to be a blast. There are pictures of him getting hot and heavy with a brunette outside a hotel—discretion went out the window years ago with him.

There's no word on whether there'll be any kind of cinema release on the movie I just made—hell, it's changed names again, so who knows when that'll see the light of day. At least I've been paid for it.

I'm so happy here, but a big part of me misses the comfort of my apartment. Sure, the security turned out to be pretty crap, but I always felt safe there, even if it was an illusion. It's been my hidey-hole for the past few years.

Cookie makes dinner, and by the time Shane and Digby come in and Ajax emerges from his room, I think I'm the only one with any energy left. The other four all look like they're about to sleep at the dinner table, and I'm not surprised when they murmur about departing for their rooms.

"I'll load the dishwasher." I stand.

"Oh no you don't." Digby says. "We'll do it."

"You haven't let me lift a finger since I've been here." I cock my head. "Inside the house, anyway. It must be my turn."

"Just let her do it," Cookie says with a yawn.

"Want some help, babe?" Shane asks.

I shake my head. "I've got it. You go take a shower."

He slides his hand around my hip and pulls me against him. "Is that your way of telling me I smell?"

I wave my hand in front of my face. "Well, now you mention it."

"No shower, no sexy times." Digby laughs.

Ajax barks out a laugh, stands, shakes his head, and disappears into the living room.

"Dude is barely alive, I tell you," Cookie says.

"I'm sure he'll be fine tomorrow." I pick up my plate and reach for Shane's. "Now, all of you, get out of here and get some sleep."

Digby and Cookie leave next. Shane stands and picks up Ajax's plate. "Are you sure you don't want some help?"

"Let me be useful." I glare at him.

He walks to the dishwasher, opens it, and slides the plate in before turning back to me. I place the dishes I'm carrying on the kitchen counter.

"Jess? Are you feeling okay?" Shane asks.

I shrug. "Just a little homesick. I took up your offer and used your computer this afternoon."

"And the world is moving on along without Jessie Lane." He wraps his arms around my waist.

"I knew it would be. It's just weird not being close to it."

Shane tilts his head and lowers his mouth over mine. His kiss is warm and familiar now. My spine tingles as his tongue skirts over my own and I melt into his arms.

I close my eyes as he laces kisses down my neck, burying his face into my hair.

"Go," I whisper. "Before I abandon the dishes to the morning and everyone gets grumpy with me."

He chuckles. "No one's going to be grumpy with you. They all love you too much."

I pat at his chest. "Get going and take that shower. I'll join you in bed."

"Now, there's a great suggestion."

After another kiss pressed to my lips, he leaves the kitchen, and I let out a sigh.

When I go home, I need to convince him to come with

me. I've let him get closer than I've ever let anyone else, and I don't want to let that go.

I don't want to let him go.

I'm still unsure if this is love, but if it's not, it must be close to it.

Maybe I need to work that out before my time here is up.

By the time I get all the dishes stacked, find the cleaning tablets, and work out how to switch the damn dishwasher on, I'm sure Shane will have finished his shower.

Sure enough, Shane sits on the bed, TV remote in his hand, flicking through the channels. He looks up and meets my gaze with a tired smile on his face.

"Has my poor baby had a long day?" I jut out my bottom lip.

"Something like that."

"Want a massage?"

One corner of his mouth tilts up. "I wouldn't say no."

I swagger toward him, crawling up the bed until I reach the pillows. "I've got a favour to ask you first."

"And that is?" He cocks an eyebrow.

"I was talking with Ajax earlier and he wants to invite this magical woman to come and meet us." I clap. "So I thought we could all have dinner."

"Fuck no." Shane crosses his arms. "No outside visitors."

"But—"

"No buts, Jessie. If Ajax wants to see her, he can go somewhere else."

I snuggle in tight against him. "Come on, Shane. I'm okay with it. You should have seen his smile earlier. She's clearly made a big impact."

"And we know nothing about her."

"Ajax says she's from Auckland but has spent time in Australia. I don't think there's anything there to ring alarm bells. Please? For me? I want to meet this woman."

His expression softens and he uncrosses his arms, slipping one around me. "I'm not happy about this."

I peck him on the cheek. "Thank you."

"For what? I didn't say yes."

Meeting his gaze, I use my free hand to run a finger along his belt.

He narrows his eyes as my hand drifts downward. "You're not playing fair."

"Life's not fair." My voice is husky. I'm not just doing this for him. I want him just as badly as he wants me. "And little Shane seems to be getting excited." Giving his cock a squeeze, I keep my gaze locked with his until he cracks a smile.

"Little Shane is always excited around you."

I unbutton his jeans and slowly slide the zip down. "You know, little Shane's not really so little. And I bet he'd love it if I put my mouth—"

"Okay. Okay." He chuckles. "Is this really *that* important to you?"

I place a palm on his chest. "I'm so happy right now. *You* make me happy. I just want Ajax to have that. He's besotted."

He studies me closely. "You make me happy too, but this? This does not make me happy. But I also know that Ajax is a grown man, and I can't stop this if you all gang up and make it happen."

"I'm still going to blow you. I was either way." I shrug. "And then I'll give you a massage."

Shane huffs out a frustrated breath. "Now you tell me."

"You're so cute when you're mad."

20

SHANE

By the time Saturday arrives, I'm still unhappy about this whole dinner arrangement.

If the investigation had gone the way it should have, Jessie would have been out of here by now with no threat hanging over her. But as her stay goes on, it gets harder and harder to ask the guys not to live their normal lives.

The one thing I do know is that they love her and will do whatever they can to protect her too. And damn, it's actually really good to see Ajax so happy.

He's seen his new girl again since the pub night, and though he's a man of few words, he has plenty to say about her and it seems she's as besotted with him as he is with her.

So when this tall blonde appears on our doorstep and squeals at the sight of him, it helps ease the discomfort I've had the past few days.

"Everyone, this is Victoria," Ajax announces. She's curled

into his side and even though everyone appears small compared to Ajax, she looks good snuggled up against him. If I didn't have Jessie, I'd be jealous.

"Hi, Victoria. I'm Jessie." Of course Jessie's the first one to welcome her with open arms. She's come a long way from the dismissive woman I met all those weeks ago.

Victoria raises her index finger to her lips. "You look so familiar."

"Jessie's a movie star." Ajax beams. "But she's here for a private trip, so we're keeping her presence a secret. That's why I asked you to sign the NDA."

He shoots me a glance. When I told him to ask her to sign it, he didn't hesitate.

Victoria's blue eyes widen. "Oh, of course. I won't say a thing."

Ajax points. "And this is Cookie, Digby, and Shane. They're my partners in the farm."

"Your farm sounds amazing." Victoria leans her head on Ajax's chest. "I can't wait to see more of it."

"Well, for now you'll have to make do with the living room." Cookie laughs. "Dinner will be ready in about ten minutes."

I take a seat in one of the big recliners and pull Jessie down onto my lap.

Ajax and Victoria drop onto one of the couches, and she snuggles into him, gazing into his eyes. Jessie leans her head against mine.

Digby grimaces and rolls his eyes at me.

Dinner can't come soon enough.

COOKIE OUTDOES HIMSELF.

The lamb he serves is perfectly cooked, a little pink and so tender it melts in your mouth. Add in the roast potatoes and steamed vegetables, and I think it's the best meal I've had in forever.

Anyone would think Ajax was out to impress.

"This isn't ...?" Jessie's gaze is fixed on Ajax.

He frowns and shakes his head. "No. They're all present and accounted for. Do you think I'd do that to you?"

She looks back at her plate. "It's not the same anymore."

"I bought it from the supermarket. It's not from our farm, Jessie." Cookie reaches over and pats her hand.

"Maybe I'll become a vegetarian."

"Nah. You like meat too much," Digby says.

I glare at him, but Jessie snorts and turns to me. "That is true."

"You've been hanging around these Neanderthals too long." I grip her shoulder.

"Who are you calling a Neanderthal?" Ajax grumbles.

Jessie slices a piece of lamb and pops it into her mouth, letting out a moan that goes straight to my cock. "Oh, this is so good. And none of you are Neanderthals."

"You called me one when we met."

She turns and pokes her tongue out at me. "That was before I knew you."

I lean over and peck her cheek before we continue eating.

The whole time, Victoria's taking us all in, and I try to

keep one eye on her. I'm still not completely comfortable with this, but she seems okay so far.

We'll see.

AFTER DINNER, Ajax and Victoria disappear into his room, and I breathe a little sight of relief.

Jessie drops onto my lap again, and the others finally join us after loading the dishwasher.

"Movie night tonight." I plant a kiss under Jessie's ear.

"What are we watching?" she asks.

"It's Digby's turn to choose." I take a deep breath into her neck. She smells of my bodywash, and there's something about knowing that she uses it that does things to me. I'm not sure we'll even make the end of the movie.

"So it'll be some Disney thing." Her tone is flat, and I look up in surprise. But laughter dances in her eyes, and her lips are curved into a big smile.

Unsurprisingly, Digby misses the whole thing. "I happen to love Disney. It's not a crime."

"She's taking the piss. Lay the Disney movie on us, man." I laugh.

Digby turns on the television. "I actually thought a change of pace would be good. Besides, I've been dying to see this, and it's finally popped up on Netflix."

Jessie looks at the screen. Her expression blanks for a moment and then she nods. "I haven't seen it either and I've always meant to."

"What is it?"

She scrubs her face with one hand. "*Coming Home*. It's a movie made by some good friends of mine."

My eyebrows rise. "The Josh Carter movie?"

She nods. "And Reece Evans. It's supposed to be an amazing film."

"And you've never seen it?"

Jessie shakes her head. "We had a falling out ... well, *I* had a falling out with Josh's wife. It's complicated."

I run my fingers along her jawline and raise her face to look into her eyes. They're usually so easy to read, but this? This is something new and awkward.

"If I tell you, you'll think less of me, and I don't want that to happen," she murmurs, dropping her gaze.

What the fuck?

"Josh's wife? So, you know Delaney Carter?" We turn to see Cookie standing behind the couch. It's like a lightbulb goes off over his head as he stares at Jessie. "I told you I watch her cooking videos, but you didn't tell me you know her."

Jessie nods slowly. "I've only seen the first video, but I hear she has quite the audience."

"She's sex on legs, that woman. Better than Nigella, I reckon."

I laugh. "Are you sure about that? I seem to remember you having a real thing for Nigella."

Cookie shrugs. "Delaney has no clue about how smoking she is. That's what makes her hot."

Jessie's gone quiet, and I look at her to see her picking at her nails. *That's different.*

"You okay?" I ask.

She blinks a bunch of times. "I ... uh .... well, she has a

very devoted husband who adores her, and she's head over heels with him."

"I can take him." Cookie puffs out his chest, and I laugh.

"She'd probably throat punch you if you so much as threatened him," Jessie says. She's smiling, but there's a sad tone to her words. There's something more going on there, but I'm not about to press her in front of the guys.

"Oh. Shit. That might be a problem." Cookie chuckles. "I'll just admire her from afar. Maybe you can introduce us."

Jessie screws up her face. "She doesn't like me, but there's no reason she won't like you."

"How can anyone not like you?" Digby's tone is dripping with sarcasm.

"Oh ha ha," Jessie replies. "Delaney has a reason not to like me. I've been avoiding apologising to her for years."

"What did you do?"

Jessie shrugs. "Nothing I'm proud of." She meets my gaze. "My life seems to be full of those moments."

A loud moan comes from the direction of Ajax's room followed by a lot of huffing and puffing noises.

"I'm not sure if those two are fucking or killing each other," Digby says before shifting his focus to me. "They're as bad as you two."

"We've never been that loud." Jessie's proclamation makes us all laugh.

"Sure you have. You do that thing where you screech like a barn owl." He winks at her.

Jessie's eyes widen, and she bursts out laughing. "I do not."

"Bray like a donkey?" His eyes are bright with amusement.

Jessie snorts.

"Snort like a pig?"

I rub her arm. "I'm glad you're laughing about that. The old Jessie would have just been angry."

Her eyes glisten with happiness. "I'm not that woman anymore."

"No. You're so much easier to live with now you don't have that stick up your butt."

Cookie holds up his hands. "We are not talking about sticking things up butts today, thank you."

Jessie laughs some more. I love that sound. It's hard to reconcile the woman in my arms with the one I met all those weeks ago. She's at home, she's relaxed and carefree, and she's mine.

I'm happier than I'd ever thought I would be.

I'd contented myself with this farm and being here for my friends, but Jessie's brought so much to my life that I never knew I needed.

That'll make it all the harder when she leaves.

I'm not under any illusion about her choosing to stay. She's ambitious, sure, but she's also damn good at her job.

Jessie Lane has the world at her feet.

We're together right now, but what else do I have to offer her?

"Are we doing this movie night?" Ajax appears, his arm slung around Victoria. They drop together onto the other sofa, and she curls herself around him.

Jessie shoots me an amused look, clamping her lips together.

We can't talk. We're cuddled up together on the recliner again, Jessie's lithe body stretched out on top of my large frame.

The movie turns out to be very different from our usual fare. But the way everyone is glued to the TV screen suggests no one wants to switch it off.

It's the story of a man who's deployed while his wife screws around with his best friend. She comes to her senses before he returns, but he's got enough to deal with as he tries to resettle into civilian life without his wife's infidelity and his friend's betrayal.

It's sweet and sad all at once, and the lead plays the main character so well, it's like he could be a returned serviceman. More than once, I have a lump in my throat.

Jessie sobs. I don't know what else to do but hold her and let her drop tears all over me. She nestles in tight against me, and I plant kisses in her hair, my eyes still glued to the screen. No wonder it won a bunch of awards.

"It was beautiful," she whispers. "Josh and Reece did themselves proud."

"That Gabby Reynolds is a looker," Digby says. "I wouldn't mind—"

"She also has a boyfriend who is head over heels in love with her. Sickeningly so."

"Do you have *any* friends back home who aren't attached?" he asks.

Jessie laughs. "I'm not sure."

"Fat lot of good you are, then." He crosses his arms.

She reaches over to the couch, picks up a cushion, and throws it at him, hitting him in the face.

"You'll miss me when I'm gone," she says.

My throat tightens at the thought.

"Where are you going?" Victoria asks.

Jessie's face falls. "Eventually, I'm going home to LA."

With the movie finished, Digby switches back to television and grumbles about how there's probably nothing on.

Jessie holds up one hand. "Stop."

"You don't watch *Grey's Anatomy*, do you?" he asks.

"Not usually, but ..." She stares at the screen for a moment and then laughs. "Oh my God. Reece Evans."

He leans forward. "It is too."

I shake my head as the pair of them sit glued to the screen. Cookie rolls his eyes and goes to the fridge for another beer, holding one up when he gets there to ask me if I want one too. I shoot him the thumbs up and he cracks two open, bringing me back a bottle.

Jessie's so animated that it's hard to look away. She laughs and claps and grins all the way through the episode.

"Are there any security issues if I call one of my friends?" she asks when the episode is over.

I frown. "No. You're not going to tell them where you are, though, are you?"

For a moment she just stares at me. "I ... I guess not?"

"It's not that I don't trust your friends, Jessie, but for your protection, the fewer people who know you're here, the better."

She leans over and plants a wet kiss on my cheek. "I

know. It's not like anyone will have noticed I've gone anywhere anyway."

I frown as she skips off to the bedroom to get her phone, her words sticking with me.

Why would no one notice her absence? She has friends. Do none of them give a damn what's going on with her?

She comes rushing in with her phone and drops back onto the chair on top of me, snuggling against my chest before holding her phone to her ear.

"Oh my God why did you not tell me you were in an episode of *Grey's Anatomy*? When did that happen?" She shrieks with laughter. "You were hilarious."

A deep voice rumbles through the phone, and my gut twists at the sound. She said it was a friend. There's no reason to think he's anything more than that, but her tone is friendly, and there's a familiarity about it that irks me.

"Oh, really? Oh my God, Reece. That's so sweet. Did you get laid?"

She laughs again.

"I don't really want to know. But that's amazing. I hope Pania knows how lucky she is. It was like watching you be you on screen."

Jessie grips my thigh and looks up at me. "I can't do coffee for a while; I'm out of town. But I'll call you when I get back. Bye."

She leans forward and drops her phone on the coffee table.

"Sorted?" I ask.

Jessie nods and wraps herself around me. "Thank you.

Reece was one of the first people I met when I finally took proper acting classes. He's special to me."

"Special? Is there something between you two?" My heart's in my throat.

She shrugs. "We've fucked a few times, but it's never been more than just sex. He's a friend. And he's very much in love with Delaney's bestie so that's been off the cards for quite a long time now."

My jaw tightens.

"Not that I'm interested in him even for sex anymore. But he'll always be my friend."

I relax a little and press a kiss to her forehead. "Then I'm glad you could speak with him. And can we please never talk about anyone else you've ever had sex with?"

She lets out a laugh. "Deal."

"Wait." We both look over at Cookie as he speaks up from his armchair seat on the other side of the room. "You had sex with Reece Evans?"

"Don't tell me you have a crush on him too." I cock an eyebrow.

He leans back in his chair. "No, but wow. Wow."

"Who else have you slept with?" Victoria asks. "Anyone else famous?"

Ajax grumbles and she blushes.

"I'm sorry, Jessie. That was hugely inappropriate. Reece Evans is hot, though."

Jessie sighs and runs a finger up my chest. "He is. But my taste has changed. Shane's way hotter."

I gaze into her eyes and take in the sight of a truly happy woman.

I'm so crazy about Jessie.
But how much longer will this last?

21

———————

JESSIE

The bedside clock tells me it's a little after two in the morning.

My stomach grumbles, and I smile to myself.

This isn't the first time—my body clock's been screwed up since I got here, and I discovered early on that Cookie always has plenty of food in the kitchen. I think increasing my physical activity has increased my appetite.

Moonlight peeps through a gap in the curtain, and I roll over to study Shane. The man sleeps like a log. A smile tugs at my lips as I give thanks that he doesn't snore.

I almost wish he did because then he wouldn't be perfect.

I'm in love with him.

The thought causes my stomach to flip and then it grumbles, and I laugh quietly to myself. I always thought I was in love with Josh, but that was nothing compared to the way I feel about Shane.

Rolling back over, I slip out of bed.

There's bound to be some of that beautiful lamb roast in the refrigerator, not to mention those crispy potatoes. My mouth waters.

Shane's changed my life—there's no denying that. In just a few short weeks, I'm more relaxed than I have been in years. I spent so long being miserable and bitter, I forgot how good it feels to just be happy.

I'd let my past suck all the joy out of my life.

For so many years, I'd thought my life was full, but it's become clear to me that I missed out on so much.

I don't see her at first, but then she clears her throat, and I peer into the dark living room until I spot the figure in the armchair.

Victoria.

"Can't sleep either?" I ask.

She stands, cocks her head, and walks toward the kitchen. "I was hoping you'd turn up."

What the fuck?

Her New Zealand accent disappears, replaced by an American one. If I had to guess, it'd be Southern California.

"I get hungry and Cookie always has food." My heart races as I make my way to the fridge. What the hell is going on? How on earth do I alert Shane that something feels wrong without tipping Victoria—or whatever the hell her name is—off? "Want to join me?"

"I think we both know what I'm here for." She rounds the counter and enters the kitchen.

Swallowing hard, I turn. One of Cookie's precious knives is out of the knife block and Victoria's pointing it straight at me.

"I guess so. Are you going to tell me why?" I ask.

Her jaw tics. "How the hell do you do it?"

"Do what?"

"Act like such a bitch and still get all the good roles. So many times I've auditioned and been asked back only to lose a role to you."

I arch an eyebrow. "I have no idea who you are."

She takes a step forward. "Emma Huntingdon."

Crossing my arms, I glare at her. "Well, Emma Huntingdon, maybe you should improve your acting skills."

Her nostrils flare.

"How did you find out I was here?" I ask.

"I'm Marilyn's roommate."

The receptionist at Marcus's office.

My throat tightens.

"She works from home sometimes. Her laptop has access to all kinds of goodies."

Oh my God.

Marcus has everything—all my details. He's essentially my next of kin, and he gets notified about all kinds of things going on both in my life and on set.

This woman has had access to a lot of information on me.

She takes a step forward. "I looked up this place, and it's all men. One of them had to get me in."

Despite my anxiety, anger rises in me at the thought of her hurting Ajax. That beautiful, gentle man doesn't deserve this.

"What a fucking bitch." I glare.

"Ajax is great. Don't get me wrong. But I hate you way more than I could ever care for him."

I shrug. "Not my fault I'm a better actress than you."

I'm not sure where the bravado has come from, and I'm not sure what my chances are—I know how heavily all the men sleep.

"You don't know what it's like to have to fight for everything. I've seen what you earn. Poor little rich girl gets it all handed to her on a plate. You don't—"

"Don't you dare tell me about myself," I hiss.

Her eyes grow wild.

"What you see is all an act that I've spent years perfecting. You don't know me. You know nothing about me." My voice gets louder in the hope someone—anyone hears me.

She snorts.

I'm not the same woman I was even a few weeks ago. I shared my deepest, darkest secrets with Shane, and doing that has left me feeling emboldened. What happened to me is nothing to be ashamed of.

"Were you fifteen years old, getting pimped out by your mother in exchange for a few local television commercials?" I take a step forward. "Or how about the weekend trips away with my so-called manager who convinced my mother that he was taking me somewhere to audition, but was really sharing me with his dirty old friends?"

I advance again without even thinking about it. She stands silent, her shoulders slumped as if what I'm telling her is getting through. I spent years being ashamed of what happened, of hiding it because I thought people would blame me. Shane taught me to see things differently.

Back then, I was a powerless teenager with no one on my side.

After that, when I had people on my side, I blew it.

But not this time.

"I ..." She blinks rapidly, and uncertainty crosses her face.

"Don't you ever tell me that I had everything handed to me on a plate. Don't you dare." I spit the words at her before I rock back on my heels as I remember she's the aggressor threatening me.

Shit.

"What the hell is going on in here?" Ajax yells, stepping into the room.

The kitchen light flicks on, and I blink at the bright light.

"Jess. What's going on, are you coming back to ...?"

I meet Shane's gaze, but my head swims as he comes in and out of focus.

"Shit," he yells. "What the fuck?"

I look down. It takes a second for me to focus on the silver handle of the carving knife lodged in my stomach. I don't need to see well to know there's a red stain creeping across my white tank.

"You stabbed me." I look back up. Her pasty white face gives me some kind of sick satisfaction. "This is nowhere near the worst thing that's ever happened to me in my life.

She struggles against Ajax's firm grip. "I did it. I really did it."

What's wrong with her? She sounds upset.

I sway.

"Call an ambulance. Please. Someone." Shane calls out, catching me as I drop backward.

"Got it." I'm not even sure whose voice that is as I fight to stay awake.

"Stay with me, Jessie. Please." Shane's arms around my back make me feel so warm and cosy. I nuzzle whatever body part of his is pressing against my face. I don't care. I want him. I want all of him.

"Got it, big man." I pat at him, but my eyelids are so heavy.

That's the last thing I register as darkness takes over.

22

SHANE

I hate hospitals.

The only time I've ever been in one has been when there's bad news.

"I swear you'll wear a hole in the floor with your pacing." Ajax tilts his head. "She'll be okay."

I swallow hard. "It's my fault."

"That's not remotely true. I fucked up. Jessie's become such a big part of the family that it's become easy to forget she's with us for protection. I should never, ever have brought anyone new into our home." Ajax sighs.

I blow out a long breath.

"She talked you into it too. I know that much," he says.

Guilt fills my gut. Jessie did persuade me, and I should have been stronger. I should have stood my ground. But I'm not sure I could have denied her anything, and that's a big problem.

"She's one of us now. Even if that's not how she started

out. I'm so sorry, Shane." Ajax grips my shoulder and gives it a squeeze.

At this point, I can't be angry. What's done is done, and all I can do now is hope and pray that Jessie will be okay. Not because she's a client, even though that's reason enough—but because I love her.

I love her.

My phone buzzes and I pull it out of my pocket and sit.

Marcus.

He's going to kill me.

I flicked him a text when we were on the way to the hospital. While I probably should have called him, all my focus was on Jessie. Now I've got time to kill while I wait, and I need to get this conversation over with.

Pressing the accept button, I raise the phone to my ear. "Marcus."

"What the hell?" Marcus yells. "You were supposed to keep her safe."

"I know."

"God damn it, Shane. Thank fuck the woman was caught, but Jessie deserved better."

"I know."

"Are *you* okay?"

His question catches me by surprise, and I fumble for words. "I ... I ..."

"She got under your skin, didn't she? Jessie has a way of doing that." His tone softens.

"I love her."

Ajax meets my gaze across the room and gives me the thumbs up.

"How does she feel?" Marcus asks.

"The same. I think. You know she can be hard to read at times."

"I know." All the anger has gone from his voice. "Have you had any updates?"

I sigh and look down the corridor in the direction they took Jessie. "Not yet, but I'll call you when I have one."

"Make sure you do." He pauses. "And Shane?"

"Yes?"

"Don't let her push you away. She's also good at digging in and ending up alone. If you love her, then just love her."

I swallow hard. "Marcus, I—"

"Call me the second you have an update."

"I will."

I want to rage. I want to punch walls and yell to the heavens.

Ajax's hand lands on my shoulder again and he grips it tight. "When she's safe, we go home and you can punch the shit out of the punching bag in the gym. Deal?"

My jaw tics, but I nod.

Cookie and Digby walk into the waiting room.

"Any news?" Cookie asks.

I shake my head. "Not yet."

Burying my head in my hands, I sigh.

This is my fault.

I let her down.

I close my eyes and offer up a prayer when I haven't prayed in years. I'd gladly sacrifice my own life for the woman I love.

"Mr Johnson?"

I look up to see the doctor at the entrance of the waiting room.

"Yes?"

She walks toward me. "Ms Lane is going to be okay. The knife missed her vital organs."

I let out a sigh of relief.

"But she lost a lot of blood. She's in recovery and you'll be able to see her once we move her to her own room."

There's a lump in my throat so big I don't know if I'll ever swallow again.

"She's okay?" I croak.

The doctor nods. "She'll be fine with a lot of rest."

"She'll be doing nothing but resting."

With a reassuring smile, the doctor turns and leaves.

"Though I'm not sure if she'll want to stick around to do it," I grumble.

"What are you talking about?" Cookie asks.

"The woman who was threatening her has been caught. There's nothing keeping Jessie here now."

"Don't say that," Digby says. "She has you."

"She came to stay with us to be safe. I failed her. And now there's no reason for her to stay."

Ajax grips my shoulder. "You and her have something special. Don't discount that."

I nod. "I know. But she can have her life back now—she should have her life back. And that means she'll leave our little bubble and go home."

We sit in silence until a nurse comes through to tell me I can see her.

"We'll wait here," Digby says.

I force a smile. "I'll try not to be too long."

"Do what you need to do." Cookie leans back in the seat and stretches out his legs. "We'll be fine."

I follow the nurse down a corridor until we come to the last door.

It's quiet inside. Jessie lies so peacefully, and I draw in a deep breath, making my way to the bed. Her eyes are closed, and I'd give anything to see them right now, even full of rage.

I tormented her about how fiery she was, and it chills me to the bone to see her so still.

"Jessie, I'm sorry. You trusted me and I let you down." Taking her hand in mine, I raise it to my cheek. "What we have ... fuck. I hope it can survive this because I feel like I've finally found something worth saving, Jess. I'm so crazy about you that I can't think straight, and it kills me that you were hurt in my home."

She shifts position, but she's still out of it. Sitting in silence, I hold her hand and stroke her hair.

"I love you, Jessie," I whisper. "I'm so consumed with guilt and I don't know how to move past it, but I need to see those beautiful eyes open."

So many things run through my mind as I sit in the quiet that make me smile. Our first meeting. When she took photos of me getting into her car. The way she stretched right in front of me before her pole-dancing class.

"Shane." Her voice is croaky, and I kiss the back of her hand.

"I'm right here."

"It's not your fault." She turns to face me and slowly opens her eyes. I've never seen such a beautiful sight.

"Of course it is. I let things get too casual. She should have never been allowed on the farm."

Jessie reaches out to touch my cheek, a peaceful smile on her lips. "I talked you into it. It's as much my fault as anyone else's. With the threat being so far away, it never occurred to me that it'd end up on our doorstep."

"You're the client, though. It's my job to make sure—"

"Shane. You and I—we're far more than that. Can we just focus on that and forget this ever happened? I want to sleep and heal and get back to the farm with you."

I bite my inner cheek. "Sure thing, sweetheart."

Her smile is so hazy, and her eyelids seem to weigh heavily again. "Will you be here when I wake up again?"

"I wouldn't be anywhere else."

23

———————

JESSIE

I thought I'd never get out of hospital. But a week later, they release me and I don't think I've ever felt as much relief as I do when we arrive back at the farm.

This place is home. Even if Shane set me up to do all the work I didn't need to in order to distract me, I've never felt as alive and fulfilled as I do when I'm here.

Being here has changed my life.

I'm not allowed to do much, and I have to rest up, but being back in this house feels so good. It's home.

Shane's being affectionate as always, but there's something missing between us that I can't quite put my finger on. There's a distance between us that wasn't there before.

I only hope that it's because I'm recovering from my injury, and that things can go back to how they were before once I'm fully recovered.

While Shane's out on the farm, I shower.

The bathroom mirror shows me a tired woman with a

saran-wrapped stomach so I don't get my bandage wet. After towelling off, I remove the wrap and take another look.

Image is everything in Hollywood. For so many years I've lived a simple life but dressed to impress. I've dieted for roles, sometimes to extremes. I've punished myself at the gym at times in the pursuit of perfection.

Now I realise how little I really gained for all that I've put myself through.

And the man I've fallen for doesn't care about any of that. He wants me even with all the baggage.

I tug on panties and a tank top and walk from the en suite to the bedroom. My phone sits on the bed, and I know I should really call Marcus while I have some quiet.

I scroll through the missed calls. There are a lot of numbers I don't recognise, which I'm guessing are journalists trying to contact me directly. Marcus has called a couple of times, but I know he's been updated by Shane as to how I'm doing. There are a bunch of calls from Reece, and I flick off a text to let him know I'll call him later and I'm doing okay.

I locate Marcus in my contacts and dial.

"Jessie. It's good to hear from you. How are you feeling?"

I cradle the phone to my ear. "Still sore, but getting better all the time."

He pauses. "I think you should know that I'm still debating whether or not to contest Shane's bill. He was doing a good job until he let the person threatening you into the house."

I flex my hand. "We're paying his bill. It wasn't his fault—I'm not blaming anyone. And I'm alive."

Marcus sighs. "Jessie, we're paying for him to—"

"I don't care. I've been just fine here all these weeks, and I'm fine now." I run my fingers through my hair. "If anyone's to blame, it's me. I crossed the line with Shane first."

"You're not the one I employed to keep one of my star clients safe."

"No, but I knew we weren't supposed to hook up while I was basically under his guard. But this place, oh my God, this place has felt like home."

He's silent. I've not opened up to Marcus about everything that happened to me, but maybe it's time to. All he knows is that before my dad stepped in, I had a rough time with my mom.

"Marcus, I've spent so long looking for the kind of peace I have here. I haven't had that in years." I bite my bottom lip. "And while I could have done without being stabbed and that bitch being in my face, I'm finally facing up to everything that happened to me when I was a kid."

"Jessie," he murmurs.

"My mother basically pimped me out for those early roles. I got a shampoo commercial at sixteen because I blew the director and not because I wanted to. And that was just one job."

He gasps.

"When I found you, I was so relieved to find a manager who didn't want to fuck me or send me on jobs where the casting requirement was sex. You sent me to real jobs with proper professionals who never took advantage of me."

"I wish I'd known."

"You changed my life, Marcus, and I repaid you by

making everything difficult. I thought the industry owed me."

"I can understand that."

"That's not me anymore. It's taken this and meeting Shane to change all that."

There's a pause. "You really do love him."

"I'm crazy about the Neanderthal. And I'm also itching to get back to work. Do you think anyone's going to cast me?"

He chuckles. "Actually, that's one of the reasons I wanted to talk to you. I've got a role lined up if you're interested. And it's a good one."

I grin. "What is it?"

The crinkling of a piece of paper comes down the phone. "I have in my hand a request for you to audition for the new Tessa Armstrong movie."

Gasping, I slam my hand over my mouth. "No. I always wanted to work with her."

"I know, and you should have been on her radar well before now. Production doesn't start for nearly another year, but they want to see you now and secure you for it."

"Marcus, she has such strong, empowered female characters in her films."

His tone softens. "That's you, Jessie. And this movie is about a group of female assassins competing in a world full of men."

"I've never made an action film."

He chuckles. "Now's your chance. If you want it. My inbox is full of queries about when you're returning to work. This incident seems to have worked magic as far as your reputation is concerned. People think you've been on edge because of the threats."

I bite my bottom lip. "That makes no sense. It's not like the threats have been going on for years."

"No one seems to know that or care. They're all in a rush to work with you because you have talent and you're in the spotlight right now. I'll look through all these and we'll see what other offers come out in the wash."

My eyes widen as Shane walks toward me. Marcus keeps talking, and it's probably important and related to my career, but Shane's warm hands on my hips make me lose concentration as he lifts me to slide down my panties.

"And then I thought ..." he continues.

My eyes roll back in my head as Shane positions his face between my legs. I rise off the bed when he goes straight in to suck my clit.

"Marcus," I gasp.

"Are you okay, Jessie?"

I run my free hand through my curls. "It's just ... I'm having some trouble focusing because ... oooh."

Shane chuckles against me and his hot breath puts me on the edge.

"Can I call you back?" I croak.

Marcus laughs. "I'll leave you two lovebirds to it and put everything in an email."

Shane pushes me back onto the bed, pushing my tank top up and kissing his way to my stomach. "My name's Shane, and I'm addicted to Jessie Lane's pussy," he murmurs.

"You did not just say that." I wag a finger at him.

"He did," Marcus says. "Talk to you later."

I throw my phone on the bed and raise my hands over my head. "Marcus heard that."

Shane plants kisses up my stomach, runs his tongue around my belly button, and slowly makes his way up until he suckles on each nipple. "I don't care."

"He's apparently got a ton of job offers for me."

He stops, raises his head, and meets my gaze. "So, back to work?"

"I nearly tanked my career with my own bad behaviour. It's my chance to get it back." I lick my lips. "Sounds like someone stalking and trying to kill me has been good for business."

Those dark eyes I love so much search mine. "And that's what you want?"

I hesitate for a moment. It'd be easy just to stay here, but I still have so many things I want to achieve, and a life waiting for me back home. "I can't walk away from my career. Not when I fought so hard for it."

He nods. "I understand that."

"You could come with me?"

Shane frowns. I don't have to ask again to know what his answer will be. His life is here. Mine is in LA. I'm not sure how to make this work, and I don't think he knows either.

He plants a kiss between my breasts. "How about we park this conversation and revisit it later?"

"Okay." I stroke his cheek. "I'm looking forward to sleeping in our bed tonight."

"Come here, then."

He climbs into bed and opens his arms. I crawl up and

under the blankets, settling on my side. He curls around me, spooning me and making me feel secure.

I love that feeling—I've felt it so rarely in my life. But Shane soothes my soul like no one else ever has.

And after a week of bad sleep in a hospital bed, I drift off without a care.

It's still dark when I wake, and the warmth against my back is gone. Long gone, judging by the cool sheets.

"Shane?" I call out.

Sliding out of bed, I walk through the quiet house.

A little more than a week ago, I could do this without a care. Now I peer around every corner, turning on and off lights as I go, even though I know there's no one there.

There's no sign of Shane.

With the light back off in the kitchen, I cast my gaze out the window.

One of the things that I've had to get used to in the country is the dark, but there's enough moonlight out there for me to make out a Shane-like shape sitting on a bench in the yard.

I open the door and shiver.

My bare feet are cool on the damp grass, but I don't care.

He turns to look over his shoulder as I approach.

"Hey." I press a kiss to the top of his head. "What are you doing out here?"

Shane pulls me down onto his lap, and I wrap my arms around his neck.

"Just needed some fresh air." He frowns. "There's something I need to talk to you about." His jaw tics and I bite my bottom lip, knowing that whatever it is isn't good. "It's time for you to go home."

I lean back a little. "Is this something to do with the call I had with Marcus?"

"He called me while you were asleep. Wanted me to make sure you were ready to go."

"Go?"

He nods. "He wants you back in LA as soon as possible. There's a whole world waiting for you and your talent."

"But what about Victoria? Emma? Whatever her real name is?"

Rubbing my back, he leans his head against mine. "She's pleading guilty. You won't have to testify and if the courts need anything, Marcus is sure you'll be able to do it by video."

I can't say anything for a moment and just let it sink in.

"Come with me," I whisper.

He pulls back, his furrowed brow telling me everything.

"You won't."

His Adam's apple bobs, and there's a painful pause before he shakes his head.

"Why not?"

He pauses. "This isn't real, Jessie. You and me. We've been living in this bubble and I failed you. What happened to you is on me."

I shake my head. "No. I was the one who insisted—"

"But I still agreed when I should have said no. I put our relationship before your safety when that was my primary reason for bringing you here." He lets out a shaky breath.

"Marcus has a helicopter picking you up tomorrow afternoon. You have a life to get back to."

No.

Don't do this.

You are my life.

"Shane. Please."

"I'm sorry, Jessie. I came out of retirement to work for Marcus, and I'm so glad I did because it led me to you. But that world isn't mine."

Tears roll down my cheeks. "It could be?"

He runs his thumb down my cheek and across my lower lip. "No, sweet. You need to go home and make the most of the opportunities you're being offered. Be the star I know you can be."

"I hate you," I whisper.

"I know."

I brush back tears. I always thought when Josh found Delaney again that my heart was broken. That was nothing in comparison to this.

Josh split my heart in two. Shane's shattering it.

"We've got tonight, Jessie. Let's make the most of it," he murmurs.

He kisses me, and I'm lost in the man who's come to mean everything to me in such a short time.

Standing, he scoops me into his arms, carries me inside and pushes the door closed with his foot.

How can I leave this?

How can I stay?

For years I've lived my cosy little existence, doing what I

wanted. Staying on the farm has opened my eyes to another world, one where I am loved and accepted, and not once have I ever felt judged by Shane or any of his friends.

I thought I'd hate it, but I've loved my time here.

I'm not sure how to say goodbye.

His kisses seem more tender than the bruising ones we've shared in the past. Rough hands caress me gently, and not once does he close his eyes. Instead, they're always meeting mine—always studying me.

He's no longer worried about me faking it, and I no longer have to. My body's so in tune with his, and my trust in him is absolute.

When I cry his name, it's because what we have together is real and magical. I'm so in love with this man.

He's mine.

And he's letting me go.

"This hurts so much." Tears prick my eyes as Shane moves between my legs.

Shane stops touching me, his eyes searching mine. "What's wrong? Where are you hurting?"

I shake my head. "Not by body. My heart."

He rolls off me, tugging me at the waist, and pulling me in tight against him. "I'm sorry."

"So am I. I thought ... I thought this meant more than just sex."

"It does."

"But you don't want me." Tears roll down my cheeks, and he kisses them away. I swat his arm with my hand, pushing him off.

"I do want you, Jessie. I just don't know how to make this

work. You have your life, and I have mine. How do we ever find the middle?"

"I don't know."

THE BED'S empty again when I wake.

After pulling on some jeans and a shirt, I make my way out to the kitchen. All four of my housemates are sitting at the table, eating breakfast.

"Jessie." Ajax is the first to speak. I nod toward him. "I hear you're going home today."

I glance at Shane and slide my hands into my back pockets. "Apparently so."

"We'll miss you," Cookie says. "Who else can I experiment on?"

Letting out a soft laugh, I take two more steps toward the kitchen before Digby stands and grasps my arm. "I'll get your coffee. Take a seat. Cookie's made a ton of pancakes for you."

"Thank you." I turn toward the table and slide into a chair between Shane and Cookie. "And pancakes for me?"

"I know you like them," Cookie says.

My eyes well up as he slides his arm around my shoulders, and I lean against him. "I like everything you cook."

He pecks me on the cheek. "Eat up. You've got a big day ahead of you."

I nod, biting down tears.

I pile my plate high then take a bite of the first fluffy pancake and moan. "I'm going to miss these. I'm going to miss all of you."

Digby places my coffee in front of me. "Hot and sweet. Like me. Just the way you like it."

I chuckle.

"You're always welcome here," Ajax says.

Shane rubs my back, and I sniff.

"Don't you make me cry," I say.

"It looks like it's too late for that," Cookie says. He reaches over and swipes a tear from my cheek.

What's happening to me?

These past few weeks I've been through so much, but I've found friends and I thought I'd found love. But I guess love isn't all it's cracked up to be.

All I know is that the thought of leaving hurts my heart.

"You guys are the best. I'm going to miss you all so much."

"Some of us more than others." Digby raises his eyebrows.

I laugh through my tears. "Maybe just a little."

Cookie nudges my elbow and I nod, getting stuck into my pancakes and knowing that this is one of the last meals I'll eat here.

It's all so sudden.

AFTER BREAKFAST and spending some time with the guys, I head to the bedroom.

And packing my things is right up there with some of the hardest things I've ever done in my life.

My phone buzzing with a call distracts me right as I zip up my bag.

Reece.

"Hey," I say.

"Why didn't you tell me what was going on? You could have come and stayed with us."

I bite my bottom lip. "No. I couldn't have and you know it."

"Of course you could. I love you, Jessie. Maybe I'm not around as much as I used to be, but you're one of the best friends I've ever had."

Swiping away a tear with my free hand, I let out a sigh. "We haven't been close in a long time. And I've been fine here. I'll see you when I get back."

"When are you coming home?" He's stressed—I can hear it in his tone. I can understand that. Despite us not being in touch as often as we used to be, it must have been hard to find out about my attack in the media.

"Reece. I'm okay. And I'll be back in LA in a couple of days. I've been staying on a farm with my ..." My boyfriend? The man I'm crazy about? "My bodyguard." I finish my sentence, but the word feels wrong. Shane's so much more than that.

He's everything.

"I don't think much of him if this person still got to you."

"I let it happen. It's a long story, but Shane's not all to blame." I sob.

"Shit. Jess." Reece's tone softens. "I'm sorry. I didn't mean to make you cry. You just sounded so okay when you called me last time and then I find out you've been dealing with all this and—"

"You worry, and I love you a lot for that. But you don't

need to. I'm fine." I flop back on the bed and stare at the ceiling.

My insides churn at the thought of leaving, but I know there's no better time for getting back on the horse than now. If I don't take advantage of the opportunities I'm being offered, then it'll be a lot harder to claw back my career.

And I do love what I do.

"When I'm back, we'll talk," I say,

"We'd better."

I smile. "Thank you for calling me, Reece. It does mean a lot."

"Reading what happened to you made me so angry. Pania sends her best wishes as well. She wanted me to let you know she's thinking of you."

Laughing, I sit up. "I bet she wanted to be the one with the knife."

"No. Don't ever think that." He sounds exasperated now. "Just come home."

"Okay. Okay."

The door opens and Shane walks in. His gaze drops to my zipped bag and back to me.

"I've gotta go, Reece. Talk to you soon."

Shane approaches me, his eyes searching mine. "You okay?"

Chewing my bottom lip, I drop the phone onto the bed and stand. "I don't want to go, but if I want to make the most of my career, I need to take this chance."

His brows knit, and he wraps his arms around my neck. "Any time you need somewhere to escape, we're here."

"I know."

"Pretty sure Digby's already building a shrine to you in the spare room."

I bury my face in Shane's chest and laugh. "Maybe I should unpack my underwear and count my panties."

He chuckles. "You probably should."

"I wish you'd change your mind," I whisper.

Shane tightens his grip. "It's not my world, sweet. And it's your turn to get your spotlight. Shine like the star you are."

"I love you." The words are out before I can stop them.

Shane lets me go, but holds onto my biceps. "Jessie, I—"

"You don't have to say it back. I just wanted to tell you."

In the distance, Cookie calls us for lunch. I think that man is trying to stuff me full before I leave, and I appreciate it more than I can say.

"Time for my last supper?" I cock my head.

Shane pulls me close and presses a kiss to my forehead before letting me go.

I leave the room without looking back.

I've done all I can. Now I'll walk away and hope that over time, Shane and I can work this out and find our way back to one another.

This whole fucked up situation pushed us together. Maybe we're not meant to be, but this is the most real relationship I've ever been in.

Shane's given me so much.

Lunch is much more subdued than breakfast was and afterward, we sit in the living room. No one says a word, but it's not uncomfortable.

It's just weird.

I look up when the whomp, whomp of the chopper sounds over the house.

Cookie squeezes my hand. "Sounds like it's time for you to go."

I lean over and press a kiss to his cheek. "Thank you for everything."

"Promise me you'll give Delaney my love," he says.

Laughing through my tears, I nod. "I'll try."

A strong hand grips my shoulder, and I look back to see Ajax. "I'll miss you, Jessie girl."

"I'll miss you too." Standing, I round the couch and fling myself into his arms. He wraps around me like a blanket and just holds me.

And then I'm pried from him and Digby hugs me tight. "Call any of us at any time if you need anything. Okay?" He kisses the top of my head.

"I will."

Shane pulls my suitcase, and I grab my bag and follow him out to where the helicopter waits. The others keep their distance as he passes my things to the pilot.

Finally, I'm left with Shane.

His eyes search mine as I gaze at him.

He presses a soft kiss to my lips, his arms tight around my waist. "Goodbye, Jessie Lane. You changed my life."

I try to blink my tears away, but it doesn't work. "You changed mine too." Taking a step back, I search out the others who are standing a couple of steps back from Shane. "You all changed my life. I love all of you."

Without meeting Shane's gaze again, I blow a kiss in their

direction and turn to meet the helicopter pilot, who guides me to my seat and closes me inside.

I press my hand to the window, watching my boys wave as we take off. Shane's the only one who doesn't, but I feel his gaze on me until we start moving away.

I'm going home to resurrect and build my career.

But I just left my heart behind.

24

———————

JESSIE

When I finally reach LA, I'm grateful that Marcus sent a car to pick me up. It's early morning, and I sink into the leather seat, closing my eyes.

But I can't fall asleep yet. I've got to visit Marcus's office.

I force my eyes open. He had my apartment cleaned while I was gone, so I can't go home until I see him and pick up new keys and get the new code.

The sooner I hit my bed, the better.

"I'll be waiting to take you to your apartment, Ms Lane," my driver says as we pull up outside the office building.

I nod toward the driver. "Thank you."

My ballet flats make no sound as I cross the lobby into Marcus's offices.

Instead of dark-haired Marilyn, a blonde with blue eyes and a wide smile greets me. I knew this was coming. Marcus fired Marilyn over the leaks that caused 'Victoria' to find out where I was, but it's still a punch in the gut to see she's gone. She was always so nice to me.

"Ms Lane. I'll let Mr Lancaster know you're here."

"Thank you ... I'm sorry. I don't know what your name is."

Her eyes widen. "Jacqui."

"Thank you, Jacqui." I take a seat and pull out my phone.

Me: I'm in LA and waiting to see Marcus.

Me: I miss you

For a few moments, I stare at the screen, willing Shane to text me back. I'm too tired to work out the time difference, so I tuck my phone back in my handbag and pick up a magazine. Josh and Delaney are on the cover, big smiles on their faces. I flick through the pages, catching enough to know that the article is about finding balance between work and home life.

I pause when I hit the photos and smile. They're sitting on the couch, their eldest child beside Josh, the youngest on Delaney's lap. My heart pangs at how much I've lost; I've never gotten to know Josh's family. We should be friends. We were friends.

I screwed that all up.

"Ms Lane? Marcus is ready for you."

"Thank you."

I stand, and make my way to Marcus's office door. He pulls it open as I get there, and I walk in and past him before he wraps his arms around me.

"I'm so glad you're back and in one piece." Marcus places a kiss in my hair, and I close my eyes against his chest.

"Me too."

He lets me out of his embrace and holds me at arm's length. "You look rested."

"Life on the farm is a whole different pace."

He grins. "I bet. That's the first time you've had away in … I don't know how long."

"Probably ever."

He nods, indicating I should sit on the couch. He sits beside me. "You didn't bring Shane back. I thought you might."

I shrug. "He belongs on the farm. Not in LA."

"Did he tell you that?"

Meeting his blue-eyed gaze, I hesitate before nodding.

"I thought so," he says gently.

I look down and start picking at my fingernails. "He's right. It wouldn't be fair to take him away from all that. It's perfect."

We sit in silence for a moment until I raise my gaze to meet his. He's studying me closely. "Are you sure being back here is what you want?"

I punch his arm lightly. "Come on, you said you have a ton of job offers. I'd be mad not to consider what's out there."

With a frown, he rises and walks to his desk, picking up a piece of paper and coming back. He hands it to me, and I scan the list, my eyes widening.

"There's a lot here."

"It's divided into potential offers that we just need to discuss from directors you've worked with before to invites to audition. Take some time to look it over and let me know what you're interested in. The planned dates to shoot are there, so you know what conflicts and isn't going to work, but there's a couple of years of solid work there at least. And no direct-to-video movies." His lips quirk into an uneven smile.

"Getting stabbed has its benefits."

Marcus snorts. "Something like that."

"I wouldn't want to go through it again."

He sighs. "When Shane called me, I was so angry that it had happened at all."

I shrug. "It was my fault. He made the right call, but I felt so safe, I thought ..."

We sit in silence for a moment, and I bite back tears. I've only been away from him a couple of days, but I miss Shane like crazy.

"I know. I did what you instructed and made sure he was paid," Marcus says.

I lean back in my seat and stare at the ceiling. "It was tempting not to come back." Looking back down, I meet Marcus's gaze again. "But I didn't work hard all these years to give up when I'm being given a second chance."

He taps my cheek. "That's my girl."

"I'll just really miss him." Tears fill my eyes, and he pulls me into his arms.

"I know you will. And that stubborn prick will miss you too. I knew I was asking him a lot when I requested he leave the farm to take care of you, so I'm not surprised he stayed, but I think there's a lot of love there."

Breathing deep, I snuggle in against him. "You know, you're like a father to me, Marcus. I'm not sure I ever tell you just how much I appreciate you."

He chuckles. "I know. You're the daughter I never had. That's why I put up with your crazy ass."

I plant a kiss on his cheek and pull away. "I'll send your list back with notes when I'm done. Thank you."

He squeezes my arm. "There are a couple of things on there that start sooner rather than later, so sometime in the next couple of days would be good."

I nod. "Sure thing."

"Oh, and Jessie? I've got the new door code and keys for you. If you're going to insist on living there, then I think you should consider talking to them about upgrading their security system." He crosses the room and opens a desk drawer before walking back, keys and a piece of paper in hand.

"Thank you. For everything." I take the items from him and tuck them into my bag.

"You're always welcome. Give me a call if you get there and don't want to stay. I can find you alternate accommodation or you can come and stay with me for a while."

I wrap my arms around his waist again and inhale deeply. For years I wished my own dad was like Marcus. Until now, I haven't appreciated just how safe he makes me feel.

Maybe I haven't shared everything with him yet, but my heart feels lighter as I make my way out of his office. There's a bounce in my step that I don't think has been there in years.

One thing at a time.

Unpacking can wait.

I throw myself on the bed and take a deep breath. It no longer smells homely here with the scent of disinfectant in the air. The cleaners went over this place with fine-tooth comb. I'm not sure my apartment has ever been this spotless.

The scent will take some time to wear off, and it's not really fun to sleep when the air smells so sterile, but I'm so tired that it takes me no time to drift off, fully clothed, face-down on my bed.

When I wake, the bedside clock tells me it's a little after three in the afternoon.

It's weird being back here. My apartment is so quiet. It's so small.

I'm feeling claustrophobic, but this is my life. I spent years living here without any problems, but now the walls are closing in.

I need to find a new place to live. There's no way I can stay.

Maybe Josh had the right idea, buying a sprawling estate with his first big money. I can afford to buy a house—nothing as big as his. But what I need is a house with a decent-sized yard. I need somewhere to breathe.

In the meantime, I'm getting out of here. Even if it's just for a little while to ease this tight feeling in my chest.

I stretch my neck, pick up my car keys, and make my way to the door.

Before I can move forward, I have to make peace with my past. Confiding in Shane helped me see that more clearly than ever. If I stand a chance of having real relationships in my life, I need to be open and honest.

Holding everything in has only ever hurt me.

It's time to put on my big girl pants and apologise to Delaney.

The sooner, the better.

25

JESSIE

I wasn't sure I'd ever be back here.

The gates are closed—just as I expected—and the security detail is obvious.

Delaney must hate this.

Things have changed a lot these past few years.

Josh got away with barely having security for years, but then he was rarely home as he travelled from movie set to movie set. Delaney and her daughter lived in a small town with all the freedom their lifestyle afforded them.

I'm not surprised about the added security, but it's jolting to see the change.

I pull up to the gate and press the call button.

"Security." A voice sounds over the intercom.

"Hi. This is Jessie Lane. I'm here to see Delaney?"

"I'll just call through and check with Mrs Carter."

My heart's in my throat until the gate slowly opens and I breathe a sigh of relief. If she wanted to, she could have refused to see me, and I have to keep that in mind as I drive up toward the house and park.

As I climb out of my car, Delaney opens the front door.

It's hard to read how she feels; her facial expression is surprisingly neutral, but as I walk up the steps, her lips spread into a cautious smile.

"Jessie Lane. What's it been? Four years?"

I grimace. If she's trying to remind me how long it's taken for me to get around to apologising, it's working. Not that I really needed reminding.

"Something like that," I mumble.

"Come in." She turns inside and I follow her. "Josh isn't due back until around dinner, and Amelia's doing her homework. Addison's having a nap, so I have some time." Her lips are drawn into a tight line. "How about I make us some coffee?"

I draw in a deep breath. "That would be nice."

She nods toward the kitchen. "Come on, then."

I climb the stairs behind her.

Glancing at the living room as I pass, I spot the pile of toys in the corner, and when I enter the kitchen, the first thing I see is the flash of bright colour from all the photos and pictures stuck to the refrigerator.

This isn't just a house anymore. It's a family home.

I breathe deep as the scent of coffee fills the room when Delaney grinds the beans. I'd always thought Josh had gone overboard with this house given it was just him, but this feels right somehow now.

"When I moved in, one of the first things I did was

upgrade the coffee machine," Delaney says. "It's so worth it for decent coffee."

"I do remember some of the best coffees I've had were when I was in New Zealand."

She peeks at me over her shoulder. "People take it very seriously. I can be a bit fussy myself."

"I don't mind you being fussy if it gets me a great coffee."

Delaney laughs. "I'll take that as a compliment."

I take a seat at the breakfast bar, dropping my bag to the floor, and breathe out a long breath. So far, so good, and we haven't got to the apology yet. I'm beginning to wonder why I felt so weird about doing this for so long. She's not a terrible person—I knew that. But chatting with her like this seems ... normal?

"Milk and sugar?" she asks.

"Black, no sugar. Please."

Delaney turns, the milk jug in her hand. "Jessie. Is this a 'no salad dressing' story because I swear ..."

I chuckle. "Okay. A little milk and one sugar."

She nods her approval and turns back to froth the milk.

When she's done, she takes the coffee to the dining table and I follow her.

I sit and take a sip of coffee. "Oh, that's so good."

"I know," she says without a hint of modesty.

I wrap my hands around the mug.

"I'm sorry." The words are hard to get out and seem woefully inadequate for the situation. My stomach twists and turns because I know it's not enough, and I have to dig a little deeper. "I was so awful to you when you and Josh got back together, and I knew he didn't want me. He never did. You were always it."

Delaney's nose twitches, and her eyelashes flutter. Are those tears she's blinking back?

"I never thought ... That is to say I didn't think I'd hear an apology from you."

I swallow hard. "You were owed it a long time ago. I was stubborn and a little afraid."

"Afraid?" Her eyebrows creep up.

"You're pretty formidable."

Her lips curl into a smile. "I'll take that as a compliment too."

"You should. Not a lot of people ever stood up to me. I probably needed them to."

Her brows knit. "What do you mean?"

"I mean maybe I wouldn't have been such a bitch if more people gave it back to me. Instead, I just found myself digging a big old hole and losing myself in it. Even reached the point where someone seriously wanted to kill me."

"So I hear."

I meet her gaze. The sympathy in her eyes makes me want to cry all over again. She's the last person I expected to get that from, but it's all there in her knitted brows and frown.

"For what it's worth, I'm glad you're safe. I read you went into hiding in New Zealand."

I can't stop my lips curling into a smile. "I did. First time I've ever stayed on a farm."

"That would have been a bit of a culture shock."

My smile widens. *The early morning starts, the smell of the cows, cleaning out the pigs, and Shane. Always Shane.* "It was at first. But it didn't take long to get used to it."

The dimple in her cheek pops as she grins. "There's a story there, I'm sure."

I clamp my lips together for a moment. "There is, but I'm not sure if I'm ready to tell it."

She nods. "That's okay. I'm not going to interrogate you. And thank you for the apology. It means a lot. And it'll mean a lot to Josh."

"I didn't apologise for him."

Her eyebrows rise.

"Everything that happened to me ... Life's too short. I've spent so long being bitter about a lot of things and taking it out on people who don't deserve it. I have to make some big changes in my life, and this was my first stop."

She tilts her head to the side, like she's drinking me in with her blue eyes. "Good for you. I can't imagine this industry is easy on women. Lord knows, I've heard stories from Gabby Reynolds.

I wriggle in my seat, her words cutting way too close to the bone. Time to change the subject. "So I noticed the security ..."

Delaney rolls her eyes. "I hate it. But we've had a couple of scares and Josh dug his heels in over it. They're not too bad really. They try and stay out of my way."

"Scares?"

She huffs out a breath. "We went out one night for pizza. Our usual family night. And then came home to find a woman in our bed."

"Oh my God." I gasp. Josh has had his fair share of

admirers over the years, but that's a bold, stupid move. Even when he wasn't with Delaney, he wasn't one to hook up with random women. Whoever she was made a big mistake.

Delaney nods slowly. "So, we come home and put the kids to bed. Josh went into the kitchen to join Pania and Reece while I went into our bedroom to wash my face." She snickers. "I turned on the bedroom light, walked into the en suite, washed my make-up off and walked back out to see this woman clutching the duvet and staring at me like I had two heads."

"What did you do?"

She bites her bottom lip. "I asked her if she was lost."

I laugh. I can't help it. I've been on the end of Delaney's bite; I wasn't lying about being scared of her. She's got a sharp tongue when she wants to use it.

"And then I told her that she needed to leave. And do you know what she said?"

I shake my head.

"She said 'I didn't think you lived here.'"

"What?"

Delaney laughs. "There are some crazy rumours about Josh and me on the Internet. She believed one of them. Anyway, she scrambled out of bed, and got half her clothes back on before running out the door. We'd just eaten pizza, but Reece was hungry again by the time we got here. Pania was about to make him some grilled cheese when it all happened." Her lips twitch into a smile. "Pania chased her down the street with a frying pan in her hand."

I gape. "No."

Delaney's face is rapidly turning red as she clamps her

lips together. And then she bursts into a loud laugh and I join her, my hand on my heart as the mental picture of Delaney's friend chasing a half-naked woman down the road fills my mind.

"Yes," she wheezes.

I snort and clap my hand over my nose. That just makes Delaney laugh harder, and before I know it, both of us are in fits of giggles.

"Anyway, I got sick of fighting Josh over security. He'd wanted it before, but I resisted it for as long as I could." She sighs. "But if someone gets that close, they could get to our girls and ..."

I place my hand over hers. "Understandable."

Her lips twitch. "Look at us, Jessie. Whoever thought we might become friends."

My heart swells. Friends are something I'm sorely in need of—especially now.

"Thank you for coming to see me." She looks up at the kitchen wall clock. "Did you want to stay for dinner? Josh will be home soon."

Should I ...?

I shake my head. "I've had a big day. He knows where I am. I'll give you the code to get into my building so you can both visit if you'd like."

She tilts her head. "I'll talk to him."

"I hope we're all good now, Delaney. I wish I'd done this sooner."

Delaney nods. "It's water under the bridge. Don't let your pride get the better of you."

My throat tightens. Pride is what brought me back to LA. Pride is what's been killing my career.

I focused so long on what I thought everyone else owed me when really, I need to get back to what I love—acting.

But I also love Shane. Not having him here is like losing a limb.

I miss him.

Is there any way for me to have both?

26

———

JESSIE

Tap, tap, tap.

I rub my face with my hands in an effort to wake up.

Life isn't fair.

I'm back in my apartment and ready to do the job I love, but it's not enough.

Two days ago, I apologised to Delaney, and then I came home and tackled Marcus's list. He's not wrong about there being some big opportunities, and as much as I'd love to do it all, I've highlighted the roles I think I'll get the most out of in terms of achieving my goals.

This time, I'll do things differently.

Tap, tap, tap.

Sliding out of bed, I pull a sweatshirt over my pyjama shirt and drag on sweatpants before making my way out to the door. Checking the peephole, I smile and open the door. "Josh?"

He runs his fingers through his hair. It's been so long since I've seen him in the flesh, and he looks more handsome than ever. And for the first time, while my chest squeezes at the sight of him, I don't get that heart leap I used to with him. I've moved on.

"Hey, Jessie. Can I come in?"

"I ... I ..." *What's wrong with me?* "Sure."

I pull the door fully open and step back to let him in.

I'm not sure what to say as I close the door and turn.

"Delaney told me you apologised."

I let out a long breath. "It was way overdue. I should have done it a long time ago."

"Yeah, you should have." He smiles and opens his arms. I fall into them and for the first time in years, I give my friend a hug.

He kisses me on the top of the head. "She told me nothing else but said you had a lot of news. I think that was her way of prompting me to come and visit. Not that she needed to." Letting me go, he sits on the couch. "Now, catch me up on your life."

"It's that simple, huh?" I sit next to him.

"It always was. She's the love of my life, Jessie. All I ever wanted was for you to accept that. I don't need you two to be best friends, but I'd like it if we could all hang out together. The way things used to be."

I study him closely. Josh always wore his heart on his sleeve when it came to Delaney, and now's no different. I didn't want to see it before.

"Anyway, I spoke to Reece and Alex before I came over. Want a part in our new movie?"

I meet his gaze. This is his peace offering, and I want it so badly. It'd put me back on track as far as my career goes, and it's a sign that he definitely wants to resurrect our friendship. That's something else I want badly.

Tears fill my eyes, and my lips tug into a smile. "I've got a few other roles I'm auditioning for, and I'm not sure about timings yet, but if we can make it work, I'd love to work with you guys."

He grins. "Good. The screenplay is done, and it's amazing. You'd be perfect for one of the main roles. I should probably make you audition ..."

Laughing, I sit beside him and grip his arm. "You probably should."

"I wouldn't do this for anyone else. You can do this, Jess. Maybe you let the fame go to your head, but you can do this role in your sleep, you're that good."

Tears well in my eyes. "Thank you. That means a lot."

Josh leans back on the couch and fixes his dark gaze on me. "You were always the most talented one out of all of us." He gently punches my arm. "But don't you dare tell Reece I said that."

I swipe my tears with my palms. "I don't think his ego could handle it."

"No way. There are days when he comes into the office and his head barely fits in the door."

I let out a loud laugh, and he grins before his eyes turn sad.

"I always loved you, Jess. Just not in the way you wanted me to."

I nod. "I know that now." Playing with my bottom lip

between my teeth, I study him for a moment. "And now I think I know what it was like for you and Delaney."

He grins. "Really?"

"I met someone. Someone who means a lot to me."

He claps his hands together. "Well, when do I get to meet them?"

I blink rapidly and look away. "He's back in New Zealand. I came home to work, but he has his own obligations."

Josh's expression tightens. "Shit. I'm sorry."

Shrugging, I fight back tears. "I'll be okay. I just need time."

"Time doesn't change things when you love someone." His brows twitch. "I should know."

I rub my face with my palm. "It's so hard."

"Yeah, it is. That's why you have to fight for what's yours."

I raise my face to meet his gaze and swallow hard. "He's half a world away."

"That doesn't mean you can't make it work."

"We live in such different worlds."

He tilts his head. "I know. But finding a love like that is so damned precious. And I'll be the first to tell you that you do whatever you can to make things right for the one you love. I'd give Delaney the world if I could."

I smile through my tears. "I'm sorry I didn't understand that."

Josh shrugs. "You weren't to know until it happened to you." His lips curl into a smile. "I'm glad it did. You deserve to be happy."

"I'm not happy, though."

"Then maybe you have some big decisions to make about your future."

I drop my gaze. He's right. What do I really want? To keep fighting for a career I'm not even sure I'm happy in or to follow my heart?

"Your friends will stand behind you, no matter what." His tone is so gentle, and tears flow down my cheeks. "Hey, it's okay. If he loves you too, then he'll wait for you to work out what you want. Trust me on that."

I look up and meet his eyes. "Things just got screwed up. He was protecting me, but I got hurt. I think he's struggling to forgive himself."

Josh nods. "I heard about what happened. Glad you're okay."

Puffing out a breath, I blow a lock of hair off my face. "It was partly my fault. I was so comfortable and happy there, I harassed Shane into letting someone into the house who turned out to be the very person he was protecting me from."

"Ouch." Josh grimaces.

"Yeah."

"Not like you to harass anyone into doing anything." His lopsided smile makes me bite my lip in an effort not to laugh.

"Stop it." I slap at him.

"You're alive and you're here. If he's smart, he'll work out that he needs to be with you. Wherever that is."

"Would you have moved to New Zealand for Delaney?"

His expression softens. "If it came to it. Reece and I set up the business here, and it would have been tough to operate from there, but if it had been the only way to get her back, I'd have moved to the moon."

I fight a smile. "You big softy."

"I'm such a lucky man. I can't even begin to tell you how it feels to come home to my family at night."

I tuck my legs underneath me. "That's what I want."

"Then go get it, tiger."

I laugh. This feels so good. To have Josh back in my life is everything. Well, almost everything.

What do I do about Shane?

EVERY TIME THE PHONE RINGS, Shane's on my mind.

We never talked about keeping in touch. I left so abruptly, we didn't really talk about anything.

But it's never him calling.

Marcus is a constant caller. When he's not checking on me, he has more news of possible roles or requests from the media wanting interviews.

"Marcus," I say as I pick up the phone one sunny afternoon three days later in Autumn. I sink down onto the couch.

"Jessie. I've got something quite unexpected for you today."

I laugh. "Given the random roles we've discussed, I've come to expect anything."

"Yes, but this is something you've already done."

Confused, I furrow my brow. "What are you talking about?"

"Your movie. *Night Moves*. That's what they called it in the end, by the way."

I laugh. "What? The hot pants movie?"

"Yes. We are never working with that company again either. Even after making it, plans were in the air over what they were doing, but your publicity has led them to decide on a limited release to theatres before it goes to streaming. It's some time away because they have to book the cinema space, but they're planning a special screening."

I facepalm.

"Now, do you want to find a date or should I find one for you?"

My mouth goes dry.

Shane.

I want Shane.

"I'll find someone."

His tone softens. "You don't need to go with anyone. It'd just be good to see you back on the red carpet looking beautiful. I'll email you the details—like everything else, it's a last-minute thrown-together kind of thing."

My cheeks redden. "Thanks, Dad."

Marcus's laugh makes me smile. It's past time I acknowledge the way I feel about him. I wouldn't be in this position if I didn't have him in my life. For years, I've thrived under his guidance—or would have if I'd dealt with my issues.

Now it's time to pay him back in spades.

"I should probably also tell you that I made up with Delaney and Josh," I say.

"Now that is good news. Should I expect an offer from Josh's production company?"

I laugh. "Maybe. He made some noises about including me in their next movie."

"I know that's what you really want. I'm so proud of you, Jessie."

"Thank you," I whisper, my chest bursting from his praise. "Anyway, I'd better go find a date for my unexpected premiere."

"Do what you have to do. Call me if you need help."

"Love you, Marcus."

"Love you too, kiddo."

MY WELL IS DRY.

Even Declan has a date and an apparently complicated story about her that I don't really want to hear even when he tries to pour his heart out to me.

Reece has Pania. Josh has Delaney. There are probably a few other people I could ask, but I also don't want anyone to get the wrong idea and think I want to sleep with them afterward.

This isn't a date.

My prayers are answered two days later with a call I nearly don't take because it's an unknown number. But after my phone rings a handful of times, I panic in case it's Shane and I miss it.

"Hello?"

"Jessie? It's Clarke."

Well, knock me over with a feather. Clarke attended the same acting class that Josh, Reece and I did. After some theatre work, he abandoned the idea of becoming a star in favour of advertising in New York. Something about being able to use his creative skills but be paid reliably.

We tried to maintain our friendship when he moved, but the physical distance between us turned out to be too much and we drifted apart. But at one time, he was like a brother to me.

It was his shoulder I cried on the first time I realised Josh wouldn't be mine. That was a long and brutal lesson to learn.

"Who?" I smile to myself.

"Oh. Don't you play games with me." He laughs. "I read about what happened. You never called me."

"You never call me, so I guess we're even."

"Meow." Clarke laughs. "I'm sorry, Jess. Life has just been a bit ... crap."

"*Your* life has been crap?"

"Point taken. How are you now?"

I puff out a long breath. "Long story. But I'm okay."

"I'm calling because I'll be in town in a couple of weeks and wanted to catch up."

Wait. "When exactly?"

When he gives me the dates, I punch the air in excitement. "Bring your tux. We have a night out planned."

SHANE

"You are the stupidest son of a bitch on the planet."

Cookie's been in my face every day since Jessie left, and he's not wrong.

I thought I could be the strong one, pushing her back to where she should be—where she'll shine. But the hole that's been left in my heart is so big, I'm not sure I'll ever be able to fill it.

"I know."

"Yeah, well, it's in print now."

I throw a couch cushion at him. "What on earth are you talking about?"

Dropping the cushion on one of the chairs, he waves a magazine in my face. "This."

Jessie Lane's new flame? The headline reads.

There's a short story all about how she recently survived an attack from someone they're calling an 'overenthusiastic fan'.

And the photo?

Jessie's never been more beautiful than when she's been in my bed, her red hair spread across my pillows, her lips swollen from kissing. But this comes a close second.

Her gown is classy and just a little revealing with a split up her thigh and her cleavage looking good enough to dive into.

But the guy beside her makes me grind my teeth.

He's the type a woman like her looks good beside. Boyish good looks and a smug smile on his face that screams he got the girl.

My girl.

"Is that who I think it is?" Digby leans in over my shoulder. "Damn, she scrubs up well. Who's the guy?"

"I don't know," I say through gritted teeth.

"Are you two ..." He drops to the seat opposite and meets my gaze. "Did you ...?"

"We didn't make any promises."

He rolls his eyes. "You've got to be kidding me. You're crazy about each other."

I set my jaw. After a moment, I give him a short, sharp nod. "Marcus made it really clear that if she wanted to build her career, she needed to take advantage now."

Digby tilts his head. "Strike while the iron's hot."

"Yeah. I didn't want to let her go, but I knew if I didn't push her, she might not grab the opportunities in front of her and then she'd have regrets."

Cookie slaps me around the head.

I shoot him a glare and shrug. "I just don't know if I can give her what she needs."

Digby pushes himself to his feet, takes the handful of steps that separate us, and sits on the other side of me on the couch. "She needs you, my friend. Do you remember how angry she was when she got here? Yeah, you were a bit of a dick to her, but she gave it back to you in spades until you both realised that you needed each other. We all saw it."

I swallow hard and focus back on the photo. She's smiling, but that smile doesn't reach all the way to her eyes. I've been under the full radiance of Jessie's smile, and that's not it. There's something missing. Still ... "I can't take time off here. You guys need me—"

"I need you here about as much as a I need a rash on my balls. You're moping around and being useless anyway. Go get your girl."

Shifting my gaze to him, I fist my hands and then release them. "What if she doesn't want me? She's just getting back on top of her career, and I don't know—"

"Stop it." Ajax stands in the doorway, his arms folded and a determined look in his eyes. "In your life, have you ever once doubted a decision you've made?"

I wriggle in my seat, searching my memories. "Not often."

"This is what it feels like—that uncertainty gnawing at your stomach. Go to her, Shane, before you lose her for good. You weren't sure about letting her go when you did, and it's eating you alive. There's only one way to find out if she's feeling the same way."

I stare at him. That might be the longest sentence anyone's ever got out of Ajax.

Digby nods. "Ajax is right. And this isn't just for you. She's *our* girl, Shane. You might have brought her into our lives, but we all welcomed her in. We all let her down, but we all love her. Maybe some more than others."

I snarl at the smirk on his face.

He guffaws. "I'm talking about you, you doofus. You love her. Go get her."

I guess I'm going to Los Angeles.

28

JESSIE

It's been a crazy few weeks back in Los Angeles.

Not only am I spoiled for choice as far as movie roles go, but Josh and Reece have invited me to be more involved in the movie Josh asked me to work on with them.

My life is completely different to the way it was before I left for New Zealand, and everything is falling into place.

Except for Shane.

There's a massive hole in my heart that I don't know I'll ever fill.

He hasn't been in contact, but then again, I haven't contacted him. I'm not sure what I would say if I called.

I miss him.

I love him.

Pulling into the parking lot outside the offices of Carter Evans Productions, I draw in a deep breath.

This is so much more than I'd ever hoped for.

My car door opens and I jump before Reece bends and smiles at me.

"Hey, you."

I shoot him a side-eye. "Were you waiting for me?"

He laughs. "Josh and I saw you from the office. You ready to meet everyone?"

"I'm looking forward to getting back to work."

He holds out a hand for me to take. "Then you've come to the right place."

I take his hand and step out of the car. Turning around, I reach in and grab my bag and phone.

"I'm really glad you're here, Jessie. It's almost like the gang's back together," Reece says.

"Find a job for Clarke and we will be."

He laughs. "It was so good to see him at your screening. But I think he's loving New York too much to come back."

Josh stands at the doorway, a large smile on his face. "Jessie. I'm so glad you could make it."

"Are you kidding? I wouldn't be anywhere else right now. What are we doing today?"

He twists his mouth like he's not sure if he should say anything. I glance at Reece.

"We're nowhere near making this movie. You're the first person we've cast," Josh says.

My mouth falls open. "You two are crazy."

Josh shrugs. "Maybe, but now you can help us with the rest of the cast."

"Don't you have a casting director for that?"

Reece takes a deep breath. "We do. We're working with a

new one and we're going to meet with him today. But we both want your opinion."

My heart swells. All I wanted was to get my friends back, but this? This is the icing on the cake. "Any chance of an executive producer credit, then?" I ask.

Josh frowns. Reece rolls his eyes.

"We'll discuss that later." Reece laughs.

The three of us walk into the office together, and pride fills my chest looking at the office of the business Josh and Reece built. Huge photos line the walls—scenes from their movies and images from their Oscar wins. Tears well in my eyes at the thought of just how much I've missed.

"Your two o'clock is here, Mr Carter." The receptionist beams. "I've taken him into the boardroom and given him coffee."

"Thanks, Melody. We'll take it from here."

"So, who is this guy?" I ask.

Neither of them answer as they push open a door to our right and step back to let me in first.

"Davis Menzies," Josh says.

What he says doesn't register at first as I'm greeted with the sight of a tall, bulked up man in a brown suit, looking out the boardroom window.

He turns.

My stomach falls.

And yet he smiles a big, fake Hollywood smile as if he doesn't recognise me. Pain rips across my chest. Maybe he doesn't. Maybe I wasn't the only one.

"Jessie?" Reece takes hold of my arm as I drop to my knees. My body battles to draw in enough air to fill my lungs, but it can't, and I'm faintly aware I'm wheezing as I struggle to catch a breath.

"Shit. Are you okay?" Josh drops down next to me, and I shake my head.

This can't be happening.

I can't see through my tears as I meet Josh's gaze. "Not him. Please."

"Out. Get out." Reece doesn't miss a beat. "I want you off this property …"

Davis holds up his hands. "I don't know what—"

"I was fifteen, you sick fuck." I draw in a breath so sharp it makes me cough, and Josh rises beside me.

Davis pales. How could he not remember? I've relived that first day over and over again right along with the rest of them in my head, yet he's walking around without a care in the world.

I swear, Josh growls. "Leave now or I'll call security."

My head's bowed when he walks out, and I pull my knees up to my chest and rock as Reece gets down on the floor beside me.

"Josh is getting rid of him. I'm right here, Jessie. He can't hurt you now. I've got you."

He wraps his arms around me as best he can, and I lean against him. "I didn't think I'd ever see him again," I whisper.

"I'm so sorry, Jess."

"My mother practically served me up on a plate." I draw in another sharp breath. Tears flood my cheeks, soak my shirt. "I was just a kid."

"If we'd known, we'd never have considered working with him. You know that, right?" He squeezes my arm.

I nod rapidly. "Of course I do. You're two of the most decent men I know."

"It doesn't feel that way right now. Not seeing you like this."

Meeting his gaze, I shake my head. "It's not your fault. You didn't know any of it."

"Jessie." A woman's voice comes from the door, and Pania drops onto the floor in front of me. "Josh told me you were in here. Can I help?" She reaches for one of my hands and gives it a squeeze.

I shake my head.

"I know you've made amends with Delaney and if she's happy, then I'm happy. So you're stuck with me now." Her smile's so warm and comforting, and I snort before slapping my hand over my nose and mouth with embarrassment.

I let out a nervous laugh.

"Let's get you out of here. Want to come back to our place?" she asks.

"You don't have to—"

"Any excuse to knock off work early." Her smile's more cautious this time. "You don't have to tell me what's going on, but let's go get a coffee. I'll call Delaney. Maybe we can go to her house. She'll have baking."

"She always has baking." Reece pats his stomach and I laugh.

"That sounds good." I sit back up straight and meet his gaze. "You believed me."

His brows knit as he frowns. "Why wouldn't I?"

"I didn't talk about it for years because I didn't think anyone would. Or that they'd think I was somehow to blame." I let out a loud sob as I suck in a big breath. "You didn't hesitate."

"Of course I didn't." His wounded tone pierces me in the heart. "You didn't even have to tell me; I saw how you reacted. I knew whatever he'd done was bad."

"Thank you," I whisper. Shane was the same—he never hesitated to believe me and take my side.

Shane.

The tears flow faster, and Reece hugs me. Pania's face is tight with tension, her dark eyes filled with concern.

All this time I felt alone, but all I had to do was reach out.

"We'll leave your car here. You can come with me." Reece places a kiss on my forehead.

"I don't know if I could drive anyway," I whisper.

He looks up at Pania. "Call Delaney and we'll all head over there."

Pania nods. "I'll do that in a second. Let's get you on your feet, Jessie."

They both support me as I stand.

The door opens again and Josh walks back in.

"Hey." Josh's smile is faint, but reassuring. "He's gone and he's not welcome back. I'm so sorry, Jessie. If I'd known …"

"It's not your fault. I should have trusted my friends to take my side."

"Of course." He grasps my forearm and gives it a squeeze. "Let's get out of here and try this again another time when we've found someone better."

I nod. "Thank you."

"We're heading to your place for Delaney's cooking," Reece says.

Josh rolls his eyes. "Who says there's anything for you?"

Reece pats Josh on the back. "You should know by now there's always something for me. Your wife takes such good care of me."

Pania snorts, and Reece spins on a dime. "You do too. I love your cooking. You know that."

I burst into laughter. "You're so whipped, Reece. It's cute."

Pania raises her hand as if to high-five me, and I just laugh harder, slapping her hand.

This is what it feels like to be surrounded by people who care—*by friends.*

My eyes well with tears again, and Pania rubs my arm.

"Let's go," she says.

WALKING INTO JOSH'S HOUSE, I close my eyes and take a deep breath.

Reece clearly knows Delaney well as the scent of fresh baking fills the house.

Beside me, Reece sniffs. "Oooh, she's made chocolate-chip cookies."

I stare at him. "How can you tell?"

He grins. "I know all her recipes by smell. Besides, it's Monday, and she usually makes a ton of cookies on Mondays for school snacks."

"Your school snacks?"

Pania laughs as she walks past me. "I like you when you harness your snarkiness for good."

"I'm trying not to be snarky at all. I kind of like not being a bitch anymore."

"Can we just get some food and you two can talk later?" Reece sets off, and we laugh at his form rapidly disappearing upstairs.

When I reach the kitchen, Delaney drops the towel in her hands and walks around the bench. The last thing I expected, even with an apology, is for her to embrace me as a friend, but she says nothing as she wraps her arms around me.

It's in that moment that I realise I haven't flinched at any of them touching me.

I knew opening up to Shane had set me free. But I hadn't realised just how free I was.

"I'm so sorry, Jessie," she whispers.

"It's not anyone's fault. None of you knew."

She lets me go, and I swallow hard, expecting to see pity in her eyes. Instead, she smiles warmly and nods. "Well, we're all here for you now. And I don't know all the details, but if you need help taking him down, then we're your gang."

Behind me, Pania laughs. "You're so cute when you act all tough."

"I've got a set of butcher knives and I'm not afraid to use them." Delaney's eyes widen and she slams her hand over her mouth. "Oh my God, Jessie. I didn't mean—"

Pania shakes her head and walks over to the kitchen table then sinks into a seat. "And that's what I like to call a Delaney-ism. I swear, you're the queen of putting your foot in it, Delaney."

Laughing, I drop onto another seat at the table. "It's fine."

"You know when a woman says she's fine that she's really not fine." Reece, who's already into the cookies sprays crumbs all over the kitchen counter as he spouts his words of wisdom.

"Well, in this case, I really am. Today has been a shock, but I'll survive. I have up until now."

Delaney claps her hands together. "I'll make some coffee and we can all move into the living room where we'll be much more comfortable."

It's obvious she's embarrassed by her gaffe, but I'm really not bothered by it. Already, it feels like the attack was a lifetime ago, and even though I thought I'd come back to a lonely life, it's been far from it.

Josh walks into the room, his phone to his ear, a grim look on his face.

"Uh-oh," Reece mutters. "That's his 'someone's gonna die' look."

"I have no problem with whatever we have to do, but I want out of that contract. We're not doing business with him," Josh says.

Reece looks at me over his shoulder. "Lawyer."

My eyes widen as I move my focus back to Josh.

He shoots me a wink before walking around the kitchen counter and kissing Delaney on the nape of her neck. "Thanks, Matt."

Delaney turns back toward him, and he hangs up the call, sliding his arms around her waist.

"Everything okay?" I ask.

"Nothing our lawyer can't handle. We signed a contract to deal with Davis, but I'm not touching him after today."

He gives Delaney another kiss and lets her go. She goes back to making the coffee while he crosses the kitchen again and leans on the other side of the counter.

"Cleary I won't make your story public—or what I know of it without your knowledge—but I will do what I can to stop others from working with him."

I gulp. "You'd do that for me?"

His brows knit. "There's no way I'm working with anyone who's acted in a predatory way. When Reece and I started this company, we wanted our ethics to be the driving factor, and we're not about to take advantage of anyone."

My lips twitch into a smile. "I know you wouldn't."

He walks around the counter until he reaches me and crouches down. "Jess, I think both Reece and I know that we're in a very different position to you. It doesn't tend to be men who are taken advantage of in this crazy world, and we'll do whatever it takes to protect the women in our lives."

"Thank you."

My head swirls with everything that's just happened.

Not only have they taken my side, they're fighting for me. I spent so long worrying that I wouldn't be believed—that I'd be blamed for the situation I'd found myself in.

Instead, my friends have my back.

The world I've returned to isn't the one I left behind—it's so much better.

29

JESSIE

Once Delaney's finished making coffee, she carries a tray of mugs into the living room and we all follow. Reece is right behind her with a large plate of cookies.

"I've got a plate of my own in the kitchen. Josh and I are leaving you ladies to talk." He shoots a wink at me as I drop onto the couch and let out a long breath.

As I pick up a cookie, all I can think of is Cookie and his experimentation on me.

"What's that smile for?" Delaney asks.

I inhale the scent of the freshly baked goods. "I met your biggest fan when I was in New Zealand."

She laughs, taking a seat next to me. "You did?"

"I can't believe I haven't told you yet. Shane, the guy I told you about? He lives on this farm with three of his friends, and one of them trained as a chef in the army. He's addicted to your videos and thinks you're the hottest thing on two legs."

Delaney blushes. "I feel honoured."

"He makes all your recipes. The boys are very well fed."

She takes a sip of coffee and closes her eyes briefly. "What's his name? I'll give him a shout-out in the next video."

I hold up my hand. "His name is Cookie. I don't even know his real name."

She grins. "Then I'll say hi to him. I'll be shooting one next week."

"Perfect."

We settle back into our seats and sip our coffee.

I look around the room and my throat tightens. I'm not sure if I'm worthy of the support I'm getting—not after everything I've done—but I'm grateful. All it docs is make me miss Shane.

He didn't ask me any questions when I told him about Davis. He put his arms around me and loved me. That was all I needed.

"You should give your guy a call," Delaney says.

I narrow my eyes. "How did you know I was thinking about him?"

She seems to fight a smile. "I know that look."

"It's just ..." I bite my bottom lip. Delaney and I have resolved things, but can I confide in her? Maybe this is a way of showing her I really do trust her. "I think it's over."

She leans a little closer. "If he doesn't want to listen, that's on him. I thought for a long time that Josh and I were over even when we had unfinished business. Maybe you should give your man a chance?"

I swallow hard. "I think Shane is the type to give second chances."

"Well, there you go. You won't know until you try." She gives me a reassuring smile and squeezes my arm before standing. "Want another coffee?"

"I'd love one. After having coffee here, I don't ever want to pay for another one."

Delaney laughs. "I'll take that as a compliment." She turns.

"Delaney?"

Pausing in the doorway, she looks back at me. "Yes?"

"I know I said sorry for what I said to you in the diner, but I was mean about your food. And that was such a big lie."

She shrugs. "I know."

"Thanks for the salad dressing that day. I needed it."

A smile spreads across her face. "I thought you might have. It'll take me a few to sort out the coffee. You should make that call."

I pick up my phone and hold it in my hands. Reaching out is hard.

"Calling your man?" Pania asks.

I look up at her and take a beat. "I was thinking about it?"

"Delaney told me you'd met someone. Do it, Jessie. Life's too short for regrets."

"Speaking from experience?" I ask.

Pania shrugs. "Reece would argue with me because he thinks he needed the time to get himself together, but I sometimes feel we wasted a couple of years when we could have just been together."

I chew my bottom lip. "I should just do it."

"Yes. Yes, you should." She points toward the French doors leading to the balcony. "Go out there if you want some privacy. You know how nosey those boys are."

I laugh when she winks. "Sure. The boys."

Making my way outside, I smile at the swing seat at one end of the balcony and take a deep breath as I sit.

It's so lovely out here. I definitely want out of my apartment and into a house where I have the space to breathe.

After scrolling through my contacts, I pause at his name before pressing call.

The line rings. And rings. Tears prick my eyes. I knew this would be hard, but what if he's ignoring me. What if ...?

"Jessie." He's out of breath. "Sorry I took so long to answer. I was in the shower."

I close my eyes. The thought of Shane wet and dripping from the shower stirs a longing inside me I've tried so hard to suppress.

"Jess? Sweet?"

Shaking my head to bring me out of my stupor, I focus back on the phone. "Sorry. It's just been a really awful day."

"What's going on?"

His tone is so gentle, I burst into tears. This wasn't what I'd expected. I didn't think he'd be angry, but I didn't think he'd be so ... caring.

"I came face to face with my past. And it made me miss you so much, and—"

"Where are you?"

I sniff. "Josh and Delaney's place."

"You made amends with them."

"I did."

"Give me their address and I'll come over."

My throat tightens. "What?"

"I came to LA to find you. What happened between us ..." He lets out a sigh. "I should never have let you go."

Tears spill down my cheeks, and I nod, even though no one can see me. "I don't want us to end."

"We'll never end, Jess. It's you and me. I was an idiot." He pauses. "Tell me where you are."

I give him the address and close my eyes again.

"I'm on my way."

PANIA TAKES one look at my dazed expression and frowns. "What's wrong?"

Delaney places a new coffee cup on the table in front of the couch and straightens up, her eyes filled with concern.

"Shane's on his way," I say.

Pania's lips curl into a smile. "Well, there you go."

"I mean, he'll be here in about in about thirty minutes."

Their mouths fall open.

"What?" Delaney gasps.

"He flew here to see me." I blink back tears. "He's getting an Uber."

"I'll let security on the gate know to let him in." Delaney crosses the room with a big smile on her face and presses a button on the wall.

"Oh, Jessie. I'm so happy for you." Pania beams.

My stomach's flipping faster than a gymnast doing a floor routine.

Pania places her hand on my shoulder. "Sit down. You have time to drink your coffee. And breathe."

All of that is easier said than done when you have a golf-ball-sized lump in your throat.

I sip my coffee while everyone else talks, and Delaney leaves the room to check on her youngest child.

She soon returns, a small child on her hip. "Jessie, I'd like you to meet Addison. Josh has just popped up to the school to pick up Amelia, and this little one just woke up from her nap."

I grin. This is the distraction I needed. The little dark-haired girl hides her face in her mother's neck and looks at me from under impossibly long eyelashes.

"She's beautiful," I say.

Delaney drops into a recliner and smothers her daughter in kisses. "She's a lot of work, but it's worth it."

Addison thrusts her thumb into her mouth and studies me closely.

This. I want this. I want it all. Whether I can have a baby of my own or not, I want a family with Shane.

I tilt my head and smile, and I'm rewarded with a shy smile back.

Josh returns a few minutes later with Amelia. The last time I saw her, she was maybe five and sitting at the counter of her mother's diner. Her long dark hair is just like Delaney's, but she has the most beautiful brown eyes just like her father. She's going to be a real heartbreaker.

"I know you. You're Jessie Lane," she announces.

I nod. "That's me."

She shoots me a bashful smile. "You made a movie with my daddy."

I'm not sure if she remembers my run-in with her mother back then. I hope she doesn't. She was there when I lost it with Delaney and brought out my inner bitch.

"I did. I've known him a real long time."

Sitting next to me, she reaches into her school bag and pulls out a notebook. "Can I get your autograph?"

Delaney cringes. "Mellie, I'm sure Jessie—"

"It's fine. I don't mind."

Josh snickers. "She just found out how much those sell for on eBay."

I take the pen and paper I'm offered. "Well, if you can get anything for mine, kiddo, then go for it."

After signing the paper, I hand it back to her. "There you go. I didn't write your name on it. I'm sure you'll get more if it doesn't have that."

She beams and Josh rolls his eyes. "Put your bag away, sweetheart, and I'll get you a snack."

The panel on the wall beside him buzzes.

"That'll be Shane," Delaney says.

"Go and open the front door, Jessie." Pania sits on the couch.

I look between all of them and then shoot off the couch and down the stairs.

As I tug open the door, my heart leaps.

Shane's dressed casually in a blue T-shirt that's stretched

across his solid chest, and black jeans. His eyes are tired, as if he hasn't had much sleep.

And he's never looked so good.

I throw myself into his arms.

"I'm here." He presses a kiss into my hair. "I see you."

Tears stream down my cheeks and I rest my face against his pecs.

"You know we're standing in someone's doorway." He chuckles, and the rumble in his chest makes me feel like I'm coming home.

I raise my face to gaze at him. "I don't care. I'm with you."

Shane tucks a lock of my hair behind my ear. "As you should be."

He bends his head, his mouth closing over mine, and he kisses me long and deep. I sigh against his mouth, not wanting the kiss to end.

"I can't believe you're here," I whisper when he lets me come up for air.

"I can't believe I ever let you go." He nuzzles my neck and I sigh.

"It's not like you had much choice."

Shane pulls back. "It's you and me against the world, Jess. It's been like that since the day we met. I won't make the same mistake twice."

"I've missed you so much."

"I love you."

A lump forms in my throat. "I love you too."

I take Shane's hands in mine. "Come and meet my friends."

"You clearly made amends with Delaney." He nods in the direction of the stairs.

"I did. We've formed a friendship of sorts."

He presses a kiss to my forehead. "I know how hard that must have been. I'm proud of you."

My heart swells. "Maybe I'm not so bad after all."

He pulls his hands free, and slings an arm around my shoulders. "You never were. Let's go and you can introduce me."

Everyone looks at us as we walk into the room, and I take a deep breath.

"Shane, this is Josh and Delaney, and over there are Reece and Pania." I look up and into the eyes of the man I love. "Everybody, this is Shane."

Amelia leaps to her feet, marches across the room, and sticks out her hand. "I'm Amelia."

Shane chuckles. His hand engulfs hers, and he shakes it gently before letting go. "Good to meet you, Amelia."

Delaney's lips are clamped together, amusement dancing in her eyes.

"Mummy said you live on a farm. There used to be farms near where we lived, but I don't remember them," Amelia says. "Do you have lambs?"

Shane drops to one knee in front of her. "In the spring, we do. And calves. Sometimes we have piglets."

Her eyes widen. "I'd like to see those. I want a pet lamb, but Mummy won't let me."

Shane shakes his head. "This city's no place for a lamb. They need lots of space."

Amelia pouts, and all I can see is Josh in her face. I

swallow down guilt over more bad behaviour from the past. When Josh first found her, I had doubts he was her father. There's no denying it now.

"If you're ever back in New Zealand, though, you can come and visit," Shane says.

Amelia spins so fast she nearly takes off. "Can we? Next time we go home?"

Home.

That's how I feel about the farm now. I fight back fresh tears that threaten at the thought of it. I'd sucked up those feelings of loss when I came back here, trying to find my feet again, but it's pointless.

There has to be a way I can have both.

I need to adapt to a new life, not one driven by this endless focus on finding approval in an industry that already chewed me up and spat me out.

A life with Shane by my side.

30

SHANE

"We need to talk."

Josh's voice makes me look up. Jessie's eyebrows rise, and I peck her on the cheek. "I think I'm going for a little male bonding time."

She rolls her eyes and smiles. "Go. They're good people."

"I know."

Reece joins us as I'm led into the kitchen by Josh.

"If you're going to ask me what my intentions are toward Jessie ..." I begin.

Reece snorts with laughter, and Josh smiles and shakes his head.

"Jessie told you what happened today, didn't she?" Josh asks.

I nod. "Yeah, she did. Thank you for taking care of her."

"She's our girl," Reece says.

My eyebrows rise. "Yeah? From what she's told me, she

hasn't been your girl in a long time. But I appreciate that things are getting better between you."

Josh and Reece exchange a glance. I get it. These guys don't know me from a bar of soap, but I was there when they weren't. Even if spending time with Jessie started out as a job, I'm in love with her and won't leave her side now.

"What Reece is trying to say is that we care. Even when we'd fallen out, we still cared. Jessie's back in our lives now, and we'll do whatever we can to support her. So, anything you need, just ask."

Josh holds out a hand, and I give it a shake. Reece follows suit.

They're not bad guys, and I know that. But Jessie's been alone a long time and this falling out between them clearly left scars.

"She'll be well taken care of. I know I don't have the wealth or the power in this town like you do, but I love Jessie, and her needs will always come first with me," I say.

Reece grips my shoulder. "Said like a man who's completely pussy whipped."

I grin. "And proud of it."

"Oh, me too," he replies.

We all laugh and Jessie pops her head in the door and narrows her gaze.

"This looks like trouble," she says.

I open my arms and she heads straight for me. Placing a kiss on her head, I tuck her in under my arm. "Just making friends."

"I'm glad," she says.

"I was also thinking that I should get you to take a photo

of me with Delaney before we leave here today." I tilt my head.

Josh raises an eyebrow and Jessie barks out a laugh.

"Shane has a roommate who has a giant crush on Delaney."

We both laugh at Josh's frown.

"Those cooking videos are apparently really hot in more ways than one," I tease.

Reece claps. "I knew it. She's a star, Joshua."

Josh finally smiles. "She is. And I'm so proud of her. But your friend is never coming near this house."

We leave him standing in the kitchen as we keep laughing and walk back into the living room to start saying our goodbyes.

It's time to get Jessie home.

AFTER WE'VE SWUNG by the hotel and grabbed my things, and I've checked out, we head to Jessie's apartment.

I say nothing as she punches in the code, and we make our way up to her home.

We won't be here for long if I have anything to do with it.

She opens the door, and I have to admire Marcus for the work he did setting this place to rights. He would have had to have some of the furniture replaced, but it looks remarkably similar to the way Jessie had it set up before.

"I can't believe you haven't moved." At the very least, I was sure my girl would have moved somewhere with better security. Just because her attacker was caught doesn't mean she's always safe.

Jessie shrugs. "I'm comfortable here." She tilts her head. "And I thought about moving—just haven't made any plans or looked for a new place yet."

She slides her arms around my neck. "Besides, I'm not sure what I want. If it's just me, then I find another apartment. If you're with me ..."

"I'm here, and you'd better get used to it." I press my forehead to hers. "Letting you go was the dumbest thing I've ever done in my life."

"Say the other thing." Her green eyes are so full of life.

"What other thing?"

Her cheeks flush like she's shy, and it's the most adorable thing ever.

"I love you," I say softly. "You know, I did tell you when you were in the hospital."

Her brows knit. "You did?"

"You were unconscious at the time."

She laughs and slaps my chest. "I thought I said it first."

"Nuh-uh."

"So. What now?" She licks her lips.

"Now, we go to your bedroom and catch up on the time we were apart."

Her expression grows serious. "How long are you really here for?"

"As long as you need me, sweetheart."

She squeals as I throw her over my shoulder, and she pounds on my back with her fists. "What are you doing?"

"Well, I thought I might just make you come all over my face and then fuck you so hard you can't walk tomorrow."

Jessie laughs. "Maybe it's just as well I have no plans for tomorrow, then."

I carry her to her room before depositing her on the bed. I tug off my shirt and throw it to the floor as she scrambles to get out of her jeans.

"Shit. Wait." I hold up a palm.

She freezes, staring at me. "What?"

"We need to slow down. I've barely even kissed you."

Jessie drops her jeans to the floor before opening her shirt and slipping it off.

I strip naked and climb into the bed beside her. "Come here, you."

Opening my arms, I close my eye as she nestles into them. This is where I belong—by her side. Being with her is the best medicine a man could ever ask for.

"We can wait if you want. You look like you need some sleep." She pats me on the chest.

"There's plenty of time for that. I don't want to slow down *that* much." I slide my hands up her back and undo the clasp on her bra.

"Oh," she says as I pull it down her arms and throw it off the end of the bed.

"This is what I've been dreaming of." I tilt her chin, claiming her mouth, making her gasp as my tongue hits hers. It's a kiss filled with longing, with need, and one that I hope conveys how I feel about her.

"Shane," she whispers, her eyes sweeping up my face once the kiss is over.

But this is just the start.

She writhes against me as I caress her all over before dropping my hand to her pussy and sliding a finger inside her.

"I missed you," I say. "Not just this, but I missed my princess of drama."

I thrust in another finger and she juts her hips forward.

As I slide my fingers in and out, she closes her eyes, seeming to lose herself in the rhythm. The scent of her sex fills the air, and I breathe it all in. I wasn't sure she'd take me back, but Jessie and me—we're meant to be.

"I want you," she whispers. "I want you inside me. I need—"

Rolling onto my back, I beckon her to climb on top of me. She grins and straddles my hips, lowering herself onto my cock.

"Take what you need, sweet. I'm all yours."

Jessie drops her head and looks up at me through her eyelashes, and I'm lost. She rolls her hips slowly, rising up slightly and then dropping back down. It feels like she's trying to squeeze every last drop out of my cock. "You're mine?" she asks.

I run my hands up her arms. "Every cell in my body belongs to you."

She slides her hands up my chest before bracing herself on my pecs. "All of this?"

"Every little bit." I let out a grunt as she tilts her hips a little farther. "Woman, you're killing me."

"That's the idea." She flutters those eyelashes at me and I'm sunk.

My body tenses as she speeds up her ride, and when her green-eyed gaze locks with mine, I lose it, my climax slamming into me.

I pull her down hard against me, claiming her mouth in a punishing kiss that leaves her moaning.

We roll together onto our sides and I slide out of her, immediately missing her warmth. Wrapping her up in my arms, I kiss her softly.

"I think I'll sleep like the dead tonight," she says.

"Haven't you been sleeping?"

She shakes her head. "Not properly. There's so much going on. I'm working with Josh and Reece, and making plans for future movies, and also trying to make sure that I get plenty of downtime and don't get swept up in pushing myself so hard again."

I study her closely. "Trying to find your balance."

"I love lying in bed talking to you," she whispers.

"I love having you in my arms again."

Her brow wrinkles and a V forms between her eyes. "Why did you come back? I thought you hated traveling."

"Do you really need to ask?"

Her lips curl into a smile. "I get that you missed me. But you were pretty adamant that this wouldn't work."

I blow out a long breath. "Well, I was wrong. I knew you would find it hard to leave the farm, but your life was waiting for you. I thought I had to give you a push."

Her nose twitches. "And now?"

"I missed the shit out of you. You brought life to that house, and my bed was cold."

Jessie laughs, nudging me with an elbow. "I'm just a bed warmer?"

"Oh no, sweetheart. You're so much more than that." I sigh. "Besides, Ajax, Cookie and Digby ganged up on me. They pointed out that I was moping around after you, but they miss you. They consider you their girl too."

She snorts. "Aww. I love those guys. But I'm only your girl."

My heart swells. "They love you, you know."

"I love them too. Just not in a wanting-to-fuck-until-we-have-no energy-left kind of way."

I laugh and she kisses my chest. "Is that right? Is there anyone you feel that way about, though?"

Her eyes glisten with happiness. "You. Today was so hard and then magically, you appeared."

"So, that Josh dude is the one you wanted all those years?"

She plants another kiss on my skin. "I was wrong. I only thought I was in love. And now I know it was nothing like it. At least, nothing like the way I feel for you."

After raising my hand to her face, I rub my thumb down her cheek. "I love you, Jessie. I don't care where we are as long as we're together."

"But the farm—"

"The farm is fine. The others can get in more help if they need it. Cookie's the one who drives most of the food products, and if we have to, we can find another partner. My place is with you."

She blinks rapidly. "I don't expect you to give it up."

I shrug. "I love those guys, but I love you more."

"You hate traveling."

Leaning over, I press a kiss to her dainty nose. "I love you more."

Tears form in her eyes. "But—"

"Are you trying to get rid of me?"

Jessie shakes her head. "No, but—"

"Stop saying but. There are no buts. It's you and me."

"Shane. I can't let you do this."

I scan her expression. Her brow's furrowed, and her eyes plead with me to stop. But I'm not about to. Jessie *is* my life. Nothing else matters. "You've fought so hard for your career and now you have another chance to fulfil your dreams. I'm not going to stand in your way, Jessie. I'll be right behind you."

Tears roll down her cheeks, and I catch them with my fingers.

"I'm so in love with you," I say.

She says nothing more but weeps against me. Streams of tears run down my chest, but I don't care. If I could offer her the world, I would, but I can't so I'll give what I can—my love and support.

"No one's ever offered to give up anything for me." She lets out a sob.

"You're worth it. You're worth everything. I only wish it were more."

All she does is cry harder, and I hold her tight.

"We'll find a way to do both," she whispers.

I barely hear her, she's so quiet.

"Whatever you want, sweet. As long as we're together, I'm pretty sure we can do anything."

31

SHANE

Nothing beats this feeling.

When I took the job looking after Jessie Lane, I never thought that I'd fall so madly in love with a woman who could barely stand the sight of me. Not that I was the problem—my job was.

But she saw past my gruff exterior and found the real me. The me who's not afraid to love Jessie and everything that comes with her.

The Jessie I met all those months ago barely resembles the Jessie I know now. The firecracker I met was all hot as hell, and she still has that spark, but there's a softer side to her that comes out more often now.

Every day, I fall a little more in love with her.

I flick through the paper as she makes a cup of morning coffee. As much as I've hated LA in the past, being with Jessie makes being in this sometimes soulless, artificial town worthwhile.

Casting director arrested

I blink before reading the headline again.

Accusations of improper behaviour have emerged against casting director Davis Menzies. The mother of a teen star has come forward to say she was told a part would be her daughter's if she had sexual intercourse with him. The hunt is now on for other victims of the fifty-seven-year-old Hollywood veteran.

"Babe. Have you seen this?" I ask.

Jessie takes a sip of coffee as she sashays across the living room toward me. She's dressed in panties and a tank top, and I'm almost tempted to throw the paper away and fuck her until she can't remember her own name.

But I can't.

At least not until we discuss this.

"What is it?" She drops onto the couch beside me, flicking her ponytail over her shoulder as she sits.

"I ... you need to read this."

Leaning forward, she takes the paper in hand as she places her coffee cup on the table. I reach over and point to the story.

"Holy shit." Her eyes widen as she skims the words. "This is ... He's still doing it. I thought ... I thought maybe it was just me. I thought ..."

She holds her hand across her mouth. I reach out and pull her closer, closing my eyes as hot tears spill down my shirt.

"You need to speak up." I rub her back.

Jessie nods. "I know," she whispers. "That poor girl. I'm so glad her mother wasn't like mine."

"I'll be right behind you, whatever you decide."

She turns her head, meeting my gaze, her eyes so full of love. "I know you will. I love you."

"I love you too. Let's nail this sucker to the wall."

Jessie giggles. "You're so hot when you get all tough."

"If it were up to me, this arsehole would suffer death by a million papercuts."

Her expression softens.

"And I'd give him every single cut. Slowly. One at a time."

"You don't need to impress me."

I shrug. "I'm not trying to. The women he's victimised need justice."

She points at the paper. "There's a number there. I should give it a call."

Placing a kiss on her temple, I hum my agreement. "You should."

"I'll do it now before I lose my nerve."

She picks up her phone from the table and dials.

And I hold her the whole time she tells them her story and sets an appointment to make a formal statement.

My woman is the bravest I've ever met.

SILENCE DESCENDS in the boardroom where Jessie's meeting Josh and Reece. This is attempt two at getting things going for their movie, and despite my initial wariness of them, I've accepted their role in Jessie's life. They seem to have accepted me too.

Even when I sit in on their meetings.

It just seems like they're on board with me being overprotective for a while. Jessie's attack was only a short time ago, so while I'll back off over time, for now, I need to be with her.

They've finished talking business.

"I saw the news article about Davis today. That'll be the final nail in the coffin as far as our contract dealings go. There's still a legal process to go through because he wanted to fight it, but our lawyer says this will play in our favour," Josh says.

Jessie fixes her gaze on me, and I nod. We're doing this as a team.

"I made some calls and added my name to the list," Jessie says.

Reece stands, walks around the table, and grips Jessie's bicep. "I'm so proud of you. That took some courage."

"Courage, she has in spades." I wink at her. Moving my chair closer to her, I slip an arm around her shoulder and pull her in tight against me, placing a kiss in her hair. She draws in a deep breath.

This is tough for her. Everything she ever wanted to bury and try to move on from is going to surface, but it's necessary. Not just for her, but for every other woman that douchebag ever touched.

"Agreed," Reece says.

"Don't hate me for what I'm about to suggest," Josh says.

I stiffen.

"Write your story, Jessie. Let it be a warning to young people who think this industry is all rainbows and lollipops. I'm not saying you should tell the world all your intimate business if you don't want to, but I just ..." His voice grows hoarse. "My daughter wants so badly to follow in my footsteps, and I'll protect her something fierce, but the thought that men like that are still out there ..."

Jessie looks down before glancing at me and then focusing on Josh. "Your girls are so lucky to have you as their father. The worst part about my story is that I never had a protector. They have you."

I take her hand in mine and squeeze it.

"Besides, Delaney's a force to be reckoned with all on her own. If Amelia follows in your footsteps, not a single person will ever be able to take advantage of her because she has two loving parents on her side. How can she fail?"

Josh nods. "You're right."

"So are you. For what it's worth, I think writing my story is a good idea. It's not something I could have done until now." She turns her head and meets my gaze. "But now ... now I know someone has my back all the time and won't ever let anything bad happen to me again."

I press a kiss to her forehead. "Proud of you," I murmur.

She blows out a long breath. "What might come out is ugly, but now I have you and my friends with me. Whatever happens, I can't lose. I have everything I've ever needed."

My chest swells when she talks like this.

She's come such a long way from the lonely, angry woman I once met.

The only way is up.

TWO DAYS LATER, she gets a call from the rest home her father's in to say he's died in his sleep. And for the first time since I met her, Jessie's eerily quiet.

She's been through so much, and this is one of her remaining ties to the past that's gone.

I'd hate to think what the impact of this loss would be on her if she were alone.

But she has me now, and I won't ever let her fall.

I bite my tongue when she wants to go out for a drive by herself, and while I'm not so worried about her safety, I do have concerns about how she'll deal with this on top of everything else that's happened lately.

She's gone for a few hours, and when she comes back it takes everything in me not to leap off the couch and hold her in my arms.

There are times when I know I have to let her come to me.

"I've been thinking," she says as she drops onto the couch and snuggles up.

"I'm sure you have."

"I want to buy a house. Not another apartment."

Well, that's not what I expected to hear. Nodding, I stroke her thigh. "Here?"

"Yes. I know we talked about traveling between here and the farm, but I want to put down roots as best as I can." She brushes her fingers under my chin, raising my face to meet her gaze. "I want a family with you—whatever form that takes."

"Marry me."

Her eyes dart back and forth as she looks at me as if she's assessing whether I'm serious or not.

"I don't want to waste any more time. I know we haven't been together that long, but I know what I want and life's too short for regrets." I shrug.

Her lips twitch into a smile. "I had someone else say that to me recently, and I tend to agree."

"The whole world's in front of us, sweetheart. I'm right behind you the whole way. I love you, Jessie."

Tears form in her eyes, and my breath catches. Spontaneity was never my thing, but it seems that I'm a different man now that I've met her.

Is she going to say no?

Still, she doesn't say a word.

"I guess today wasn't a good day to come out with this."

Jessie opens her mouth, then closes it again. All it does is make the anticipation worse. "Yes. Yes, I'll marry you."

It takes a moment before her words sink in.

I wrap my arms around her and pull her close, breathing in the scent of her warm skin.

"I love you, Shane. I want everything with you."

"We don't have to get married straight away. You've got so much on your plate right now that I can't expect you to drop it all."

She pulls back. "Have I ever told you just how perfect you are for me?"

I push a stray lock of hair behind her ear. "About as perfect as you are for me."

Jessie scrunches up her nose. "You're so patient with me. I know I come with a lot of baggage—"

I shake my head. "There's nothing in that baggage that we can't work through together."

"You make me feel secure. For the first time in my life I have a real partner."

As I pull her in tight against me, she relaxes into my arms. We've got some big things to deal with in the next few months, but together we can do anything.

32

JESSIE

One year later

I take a deep breath, smooth my dress over my stomach, and smile. I've been to so many award shows, premieres, and events. But this is the most important one of all.

And best of all, Shane will be beside me.

A soft tap on the door pulls me out of my thoughts, and I look up. "Come in."

Delaney pokes her head around the door and her eyes widen. "You look amazing."

She takes a step inside.

My gown is a wonder. But then again, everything Pania designs looks amazing. I should know. She makes all my formalwear now, and her label has taken off among the Hollywood elite.

Best of all, she's my friend.

Delaney, Pania, and their friend, Lana, had a sisterhood of three. It took time, but they expanded it to include me, and I wouldn't throw my newfound relationships away for anything.

They all know my story, and while I spent all those years thinking people would be disgusted by what happened to me, they're on my side and love and support me no matter what.

That's what true friendship is all about.

Delaney swirls a finger in the air, and I twirl.

"Damn. That fits you like a glove. My girl does such great work."

"She does." I reach for her hands. "Thank you. For everything. I'm so glad we're friends now."

Delaney cocks her head. "Me too. The boys are already out on the lawn. Pania and Lana are downstairs." A smile spreads across her face as she drops my hands and links her arm with mine. "Let's get going. We don't want to be late."

My heart races. "It's really happening."

Delaney meets my gaze. This past year we've found common ground and formed a firm friendship—one I'd never thought would happen. It's enough to bring tears to my eyes.

"No crying yet. That can wait until after the ceremony," she says.

I swallow and nod.

"Let's get you married, Ms Lane."

REECE LOOKS up as I make my way down the stairs, and lets out a low wolf whistle. "You look beautiful."

"Thank you." I take the arm he offers me.

Delaney pulls away, patting my hand as she goes. "Good luck."

Reece smiles at me. "He's a good one, Jess. I'm so happy for you."

I draw in a deep breath. I'm on the verge of crying out of sheer happiness. My heart is so full. "I'm not sure what I did to deserve him, but I finally believe in happy endings."

He reaches with his free hand and swipes a tear from my cheek. "You deserve it, sweetheart."

"I don't know what I'd ever do without your friendship, Reece. You've been my constant, even when things weren't good with Josh and me."

His lips wobble like he's about to cry. "Always." He takes a deep breath and pulls himself up to his full height, and that luminous smile reappears. "Time to get you hitched."

He leads me out the back of the house and around the pool to where a small congregation is gathered.

Delaney and Josh offered up their house for a wedding venue, and it's wonderful. I didn't want to have something big and public. This is perfect for our intimate event.

All my boys are here. Digby, Cookie, and Ajax arrived on a flight two days ago. They almost make up for my dad not making it this far with me, although truth be told, I lost him a few years ago.

He might have been terrible at the time, but he stepped up

and freed me to a certain extent. Shane's helped me the rest of the way. I'm seeing a therapist once a month to work through my past, and that might just making a difference in my relationship.

I also know Shane loves me unconditionally.

This past year, he's sacrificed a lot for me. He's been by my side while I've been filming, and as time has gone on, we've been working toward finding the balance between our two very different lives. It all takes time, but as we want to spend the rest of our lives together, we have the time to take.

We reach the end of the small aisle, and I smile to myself as Delaney makes her way to her seat, Cookie's eyes glued on her the whole way.

"You ready for this?" Reece murmurs.

"I feel like I've been waiting my whole life."

We start the walk toward Shane, and his eyes are filled with so much love as we approach. He's all I see.

When we reach him, he blows out a long, audible breath, and I smile.

"I ... I ..." In all the time I've known Shane, I've never seen him flustered. Now he wrings his hands together, his cheeks are flushed pink, and his mouth flaps like a fish. "You look incredible, Jessie."

"I love you."

He beams. "I love you too."

"Let's get married."

Shane leans over and gives me a tender kiss.

"You're supposed to wait until the end of the ceremony for that, bud," Reece says.

I laugh. "Sorry, Reece. I forgot you were there."

"Some friend you turned out to be." He chuckles and leans in, kissing me on the cheek. "Good luck with her, Shane. You'll need it."

He steps back and sits beside Pania, taking her hand in his.

Until today, I never felt truly loved. But as I exchange vows with Shane, my heart swells, overflowing with the knowledge that I'm his and he's mine.

For life.

When we're declared man and wife, he swoops me into his arms and kisses me hard. Whoops and catcalls come from our small crowd, and I pull him down to press my forehead against his.

Life is perfect.

Investigators are still gathering evidence about Davis Menzies and his casting couch. All this time, I'd thought I was alone, but I was one of dozens of teenagers and young women he victimised. Time will tell what happens to him, but the sense of relief in coming forward and doing my part has taken a huge weight off my mind that had been there for years.

I can never forgive my mother for what she did to me.

But now I have a family—one that will never treat me badly or let me down. The friends I have now will support me whatever the future holds.

And it's such a bright future now.

I've let go of everything my mother instilled in me—I know I have talent, and the movie I've made with Josh and Reece's company will do great, and that's enough. I don't have to be the biggest star in Hollywood—now I get to just be me.

With Shane by my side.

Our celebration tonight is just the start. Tomorrow, we jump on a plane, honeymoon for a week, and then fly to New Zealand to do this all over again on the farm.

Not every story has a happy ending.

I get two.

And I can't wait.

OUR RECEPTION IS JUST as lovely as our wedding.

Held downstairs in Josh and Delaney's house, we have cake and dancing and drinking.

It's magical and something I never thought I'd have.

Josh grinds his teeth so hard, I snicker when I hear it.

"What?" he barks.

"Jealousy suits you."

"I'm not jealous." He turns his head and glares at me.

"Of course you are. But you also know how much she loves you."

Cookie has dominated conversation with Delaney today. When our boys arrived on a flight two days ago, all he could talk about was meeting her. Now they sit in a corner in deep conversation. I know they're talking cooking —Delaney wouldn't cross any lines. But Cookie's so starstruck by her, and his adoration is written all over his face.

"I know she loves me, but it's ..." Josh sighs. "I'm not used to this. Do you think this is what it's like for her when I meet fans?"

I lean my head on his shoulder. "I think this is exactly what it's like. You think she enjoys women ignoring her while they throw themselves at you?"

He says nothing for a moment. "I'm mindful of what happens when we go out. And I always make sure my attention is on her in some way. I'll slip an arm around her waist if I'm approached or include her in conversation."

I raise my head. "So, you're feeling neglected."

He turns to look at me.

I poke his chest with my index finger. "You're her person, Josh. Tonight, Cookie will go back to his hotel and you get to go have unbridled hot sex with the luscious Delaney."

A grin lights up his face. "I do, don't I?"

"Yes, and there's nothing stopping you right now from joining their conversation. Go give your wife a kiss and show everyone just how much you love her." I nudge his arm. "I know you're dying to."

Josh pecks me on the cheek. "Good advice, Mrs Johnson."

He takes off across the room, ducking around Lana and her husband, Alex, who are all loved up in the middle of the dance floor, and making his way to his wife.

Delaney's face lights up as he approaches. It used to hurt to think of them together, but seeing them like this warms my heart. They're so in tune with each other, it's sickening, but at the same time, I love it.

It's how I feel about Shane.

"Everything okay?" Shane walks toward me, twirling his wine glass stem in his fingers.

"Just Josh getting a little jealous over Cookie."

He chuckles. "I don't blame him. I'm surprised Cookie hasn't attempted to throw her over his shoulder and carry her out of here, the way he's looking at her."

I stand, pluck my husband's wine glass out of his hand, place it on a nearby table, and take his hands in mine. "While I don't think that'll happen, I wouldn't object if you tried that with your wife."

Shane grins.

I laugh as he bends over and does just that. "I'm so far off the ground up here, I think I just developed a fear of heights."

He slaps me on the butt, and I lift my head to see everyone looking at us. Delaney's now curled around Josh, his arm hooked around her neck, and the two of them are watching us and laughing.

Pania holds her fingers to her mouth and lets out a loud whistle.

Shane carries me out, waving goodbye to everyone until we reach the cooler night air and the car waiting for us out the front of the house.

We're on our way to a night in a hotel before we spend a week in Hawaii at Reece's house.

Marcus insisted on booking us a night in the Waldorf Astoria Presidential Penthouse Suite, and it's the most insanely luxurious room I've ever seen. There's no way I'd pay for a room like this myself. It's not like we'll be spending much time here, and chances are all our time will be spent in bed.

Sex between us just gets better and better.

It's probably because Shane wants to devour me every time we set foot in the bedroom, and the living room, and occasionally the kitchen. Oh, and then there's the shower …

"This is amazing." I take in the view of Beverly Hills while Shane preoccupies himself with nuzzling my neck from behind.

"Yes, yes, it is."

"I meant the room."

"I meant my wife." He places his hands on my shoulders, brushing across my skin until he reaches the top of my zipper.

"I wanted little buttons down the back, but Pania pointed out a zip would be faster."

His eyes glisten with amusement. "She's a wise woman."

I hold my breath as he slowly runs the zipper down, peeling open the dress and revealing my back.

"God damn it, Jessie, you're so beautiful." He slides the fabric over my arms until the dress pools at my feet.

I turn around, and he takes in the sight of me in a white lace bodysuit complete with suspenders and stockings.

Shrugging one shoulder, I push at the fabric to remove the suit.

"Fuck no. You are keeping that on. Even the heels," he says.

My eyes widen. "Oh, Mr Johnson."

"Don't you Mr Johnson me, woman." He chuckles. "Up until now, the best idea I ever had was installing a pole in our bedroom. This is right up there with it."

I laugh. Our house has such a big master bedroom that Shane surprised me last Christmas by having a pole installed. It's still a great workout, but it has benefits way beyond that.

As I guide his hand between my legs, his eyes light up as he finds the poppers on my bodysuit between him and my pussy.

"Easy to open. You thought of everything."

"I'm working on being a good wife."

He scoops me up and deposits me on the bed. "Scoot up to the pillows. I want to bury my face in your pussy with your legs around my neck."

I push myself backward, thanking myself for the flexibility working on the pole gives me. He's right behind me and has removed his shirt. His large fingers open the poppers. Hunger crosses his handsome features, and I don't get a chance to pause before he flattens his tongue and licks my pussy.

"Shane," I gasp.

"I fucking love this pussy. No matter how much I get of it, I want more."

I giggle, and he tongues my clit, his hands sliding up my legs. Taking the hint, I wrap them around his neck.

"Hell, I dreamed about those long legs long before we were together. Seeing you in hot pants every day while you made that movie was damn hard."

"Oh, my poor baby." I reach down and push his head back to work.

His tongue swirls around my clit. I close my eyes as he slides one finger into me, then another. Rocking my hips against him, I ride his fingers until I cry out his name, my body convulsing in pleasure.

"Jessie." He pushes himself up. "Look at me."

Opening my eyes, I watch as he rises above me, fisting his cock. I drop my legs back onto the bed, and he pushes inside me with a grunt.

"I love you," he says as he tugs at my body suit, pulling it down until my right breast is exposed.

"I love you," he says as he thrusts hard into me, filling me up as only he can.

"I love you." He licks my nipple before sucking it into his mouth, his hands stroking my thighs and pulling me in tighter against him.

I run my hands up his chest when he raises his head to kiss me. Our tongues move in unison with each of his thrusts, my hips rising to meet him. I've never been so in harmony with another person.

"You'll be the death of me, Jessie Johnson." He lets out a loud groan, spilling into me, and holds me tight against him as he rolls to my side, still buried inside me. "I'm the luckiest man on the planet."

"I'm the lucky one."

He runs his thumb down my cheek and across my lip. "I love you," he says. "I think I loved you from the moment you called me a Neanderthal."

"I thought you were hot the moment you stood in that doorway."

He places a kiss below my ear. "My favourite moment was you in that pole-dancing class."

I let out a sigh. "When I ran into you dressed only in a towel."

Shane's eyes search mine. "It's those moments we need to hold onto. For the tough times."

I push myself up until I'm leaning on his chest. "What tough times?"

"Marriage isn't all champagne and romantic moments."

"I know that. But ..." I run my index finger down his chest. "... we have love, and that's more than a lot of other people have."

He brushes a stray lock of my hair back. "We have loads of it."

"We do." I place a kiss on his pec. "We'll live a life that we both enjoy and that gives us everything we need, and we'll always have each other."

"Always," he whispers. "Now, ride my cock again, wife"

I laugh at his grin.

Who am I to say no?

EPILOGUE
SHANE

One year later

Our time is now split between wherever Jessie's filming and the farm.

We're learning to take things as they come, and she weighs up each offer not only considering how it will impact her career, but how it affects us.

There's a lot of give and take from both of us, but I'd do anything to make my wife happy, and if she wanted to film all year round, I'd support her.

She knows that, yet she understands my need for the space and peace we find on the farm.

Jessie's career has taken on another life. She's not having to take roles in direct-to-DVD movies anymore—the world has become her oyster since she started working with Josh and Reece.

The movie she made under their production company did well, and she was nominated for an Academy Award. When she didn't win, I'd thought it would hit her hard, but she took it in her stride and now she's working on her next movie, and it could be even bigger than the last.

But the size of the production isn't as big a motivator as it used to be. She's still ambitious, but now she has her friends and family. There's more to Jessie's life than there ever was before.

There was no case she could take against Davis Menzies. The statute of limitations had run out, but her testimony backing up his other more recent victims helped put him away. Doing that allowed her to finally put the past behind her. There'll always be the memories of what happened, which she'll never get rid of, but now she knows she's loved no matter what and always will be.

She also put pen to paper and told her story. All of it.

Her book caused a feeding frenzy with multiple publishers bidding for it, and then it shot to the top of the bestseller charts, adding a new string to her bow.

And now, one sunny afternoon in August, we step out of her trailer. Another week of filming and we'll be back on the farm for the next few months for the lambing. It's turned out to be Jessie's favourite time of the year.

"I heard Josh Carter cast his daughter in his new movie. If that's not nepotism, I don't know what is," a voice from around the corner says. Laughter from multiple people drifts our way and Jessie draws herself up straight.

She keeps her inner diva in check these days, but God, how I love my wife when her claws come out.

I trail in her wake as she stamps her way around the corner and finds a group of extras talking.

Her friendships are firmly cemented now, and she doesn't tolerate trash talk about anyone in our circle.

"Do you want to know who the last person Josh Carter personally cast in a movie was?" Her hands are fisted.

Seeing her like this makes me horny as hell.

There's silence.

"It was me. And he must have good taste because I got an Oscar nomination for that role. And furthermore ..." She stops to catch her breath. "He works with casting agents for his movies now to avoid people casting aspersions. Amelia Carter is going to outdo her father, she's that talented. Mark my words."

They just stare at her with big eyes, and I smirk.

That's my woman.

"That girl has more talent in her little finger than any of you. And she's not even ten years old." Jessie sticks her nose in the air before turning back to me and holding out her hand.

"Bitch," one of the guys murmurs.

"And proud of it," she says, flipping him the bird.

I slip my hand in hers and give it a squeeze as we walk toward the food truck. "That was hot," I say.

Her mask slips and she beams that beautiful smile at me. "I'm sorry I brought out my catty side."

"You were magnificent, my love." I bring her hand to my lips and kiss it.

Jessie laughs, and it's as magical a sound as it was the first time I heard it. "I'm glad you approve. That's something Amelia's going to have to fight all the way through her career if this is the path she takes."

"If that's the worst she has to face, then I'm sure she'll be fine." I slip my arm around Jessie's shoulder and pull her closer. "With friends like you on her side, she can't fail."

Jessie glances at me, and there seems to be tears in her eyes.

She comes to a stop.

"How much do you love me?" she asks.

"With every beat of my heart." I pause. *What if this is a trap?* "Wait. Is that a rhetorical question?"

Jessie grins. "I just got an email confirming a surprise getaway for us before we go back home."

Home. It never fails to warm my heart when she refers to the farm that way.

"Did you now?" I ask.

She cocks her head. "Two whole weeks at Reece's house in Hawaii before lambing starts."

"Sounds great." I smile. "You, me, that tiny white bikini you have in your drawer ..."

Jessie slaps my arm. "We're celebrating."

"What are we celebrating?"

She bites her bottom lip. "I sold the movie rights to my story."

I slip my arms around her waist. "What? That's amazing. I had no idea that's what you were planning."

"They approached me with an obscene offer. With that and my last few pay days, we could spend some money on the farm. Maybe build a house of our own." She throws her arms around my neck. "And ... I'm thinking of giving up acting for a while."

"Oh?" I frown. This doesn't sound like her at all. A couple of years ago, the thought of walking away from this would have caused her too much pain after everything she'd been through.

"Not forever. But I want to be a good mother, and ..."

I take a moment for her words to sink in. Her expressions straightens and she looks at me from under her lashes.

"You're pregnant?"

Her whole face lights up. "I've been trying to work out how to tell you. Are you okay with that?"

"Better than okay." I run my hands up her spine. "I guess that answers the question about whether you can have children or not."

"It was okay if I couldn't." She sighs. "But then I'd never met a man I wanted everything with until I met you."

"I love you." I search her eyes, and all I see is her happiness.

"I love you too. And our family. Just wait until my boys find out they'll be uncles."

Groaning, I shake my head. "Ajax will be beside himself."

Jessie laughs. "He'll probably want to be at the birth."

"No. Never going to happen. He can stick to his sheep."

Jessie's snort makes me laugh. I love this woman with every cell in my body.

I'll forever be grateful to Marcus for bringing us together. After a rocky start, Jessie and I have made a damn good team.

Whatever we do in future, we'll do together.

Forever.

ALSO BY WENDY SMITH

Coming Home

Doctor's Orders

Baker's Dozen

Hunter's Mark

Teacher's Pet

A Very Campbell Christmas

Fall and Rise Duet

Falling

Rising

Fall and Rise - The Complete Duet

The Aeon Series

Game On

Build a Nerd

Bar None

Hollywood Kiwis Series

Common Ground

Even Ground

Under Ground

Rocky Ground

Solid Ground

ABOUT THE AUTHOR

Wendy Smith is a multi-platform bestselling author, whose book In the End, written as Ariadne Wayne, was named one of Apple's best books of 2017. All her stories come with a quirky sense of humour, and she cries over everything.

Find me online
www.wendysmith.co.nz
wendy@wendysmith.co.nz